THEODYSSEY

Book 2
Libertania

I K Dirac

ISBN 978-1-84-327929-7

Cover Design Patrick T Coyne

The Racing House Press
20 Cambridge Drive
London SE12 8AJ, UK
www.racinghouse.co.uk
info@racinghouse.co.uk

Book 2

Libertania

The Theodyssey Trilogy

Book 1. Privateer
Book 2. Libertania
Book 3. Utrophia

1

Planet Libertania is regarded by almost all realtors as possibly the least desirable piece of real estate in the Galaxy. It languishes at the very edge of its most unfashionable spiral arm, in the company of white dwarfs and red giants, stars well past their prime – and, in the case of the myriad brown dwarfs that infest the region, objects that never had a prime in the first place. It never managed to earn descriptions like "up and coming", "lots of potential", "sure to be the next big thing" or "ideal for the trail blazer". Except once.

One enterprising developer decided that this was his final opportunity to hit the big time, after a career distinguished by spectacular crashes, bankruptcies and fraud. He managed to convince a couple of equally shady financiers that this was the ideal way to launder some of their dubious gains and make themselves even greater fortunes in the process. So he commissioned a construction firm of less than spotless reputation to begin terraforming. Within a decade, the results looked very promising. The atmosphere was benign, the land fertile, the oceans relatively calm. Plants grew in profusion; animals multiplied prodigiously. He christened it Planet Avalon, "The Land of Myth Made Real". Soon he was selling large numbers of exclusive developments off-plan to the rich and adventurous of other planets, who wanted somewhere "to get away from it all".

They soon found that they were getting away *to* it all. The planet's parent star turned out to be an irregular variable that alternated between periods of stability and intervals of stellar irascibility. The occupants of their extravagant dwellings found themselves subjected to unbearably hot summers and cryogenic winters, followed within a year or two by freezing summers and tropical winters. The magnificent vegetation, sourced from all over the Galaxy, proved incapable of coping with the conditions and expired. Only the toughest grasses, bracken and scrub, most of which had come in accidentally as contaminants, survived. The introduced fauna suffered a similar fate. The main survivors were small rat-like creatures, which rapidly diversified to fill the vacant ecological niches. Some grew large; others became carnivorous. It was projected that within a hundred generations some would be as large as horses. The invertebrate ecosystem also became utterly unbalanced. There were episodic plagues of flies, mosquitoes, spiders, hornets, locusts, weevils and scorpions, depending on the climatic conditions. The result was that the rich and adventurous left as quickly as they had come, abandoning their expensively-acquired homesteads.

The developers soon went bankrupt, and a series of liquidation agents and courts tried in vain to find someone to take the assets off their hands. Eventually, the planet was written off and left to languish, obscure and unwanted. No empire, federation, monarchy or any other entity would contemplate acquiring it, on the grounds that its upkeep would be far more than it could ever be worth. Only those sufficiently desperate or unsound of mind would go there. Or so it was thought.

The obscure and the unwanted would always have attractions for those who seek obscurity and were wanted for reasons other than affection. Pirates, outlaws, freebooters and others of a less than law-abiding disposition were quick to take advantage of its very undesirability in the eyes of others. Renegades from all over the Galaxy flocked to its insalubrious shores to get away from the tiresome restrictions of laws and the agencies that attempted to enforce them. After them came the camp-followers and the hangers-on, the flotsam and jetsam of the Galaxy. Soon, many of its old haunts had returned to a bustling, if chaotic, street life. In an uncharacteristic display of harmony, the denizens decided to establish a self-governing planetary republic. They renamed the planet Libertania, and named their capital Davy Jones, after the custodian of drowned sailors, known by his saucer eyes, his three rows of teeth, his horns and tail, and the blue smoke that issued from his nostrils.

Naturally, Planet Libertania was the source and repository of innumerable rumours, myths, legends, conspiracy theories and lies, the more unlikely the better. Truth, whatever it might be, was not highly regarded there. Those claiming to possess it were likely to be thought of as bores and would be forced to buy a round of drinks for all present. Nevertheless, whether by accident or not, some of the tales that abounded were grounded in fact, but those wishing to find out which, had to be prepared to stand a lot of drinks in doing so.

An extract from Lonely Planets, *the memoirs of Gaudi Brandeschi, interstellar traveller and troubadour. The book is banned in all but a few Galactic jurisdictions on grounds ranging from criminal sedition, blasphemy and salacious recitation to lèse-majesté. Numerous arrest warrants for Brandeschi are extant. His current whereabouts are unknown.*

Captain Sir Sechaverell Horatio Frobisher de la Beche, *bart,* master of the privateer HMS *Bountiful,* gazed vexedly at the various screens on the Bridge of his ship. He was wearing an outfit he considered particularly suited for travel to an unknown and possibly dangerous destination – flared cerise pantaloons gathered at the ankles over heavy, studded boots and an opaline, ruched blouse under a cutaway camouflage jacket. Among the reasons for his vexation was that he could see no prospect of danger – or, indeed, of anything.

"Would you be so good as to tell us what is happening, McTavish?"

A figure in a kilt of maroon, mauve, orange and olive chequered patterning, tam o'shanter slightly awry, floated over and peered at the screens.

"Ah would have thought it would be obvious even tae the likes of ye, Captain. Ye're caught in the airse end o' hyperspace because the ship has nae idea where tae go."

De la Beche gave a snort.

"What do you mean, no idea where to go? I told it to go to Libertania. Isn't that enough? How many Libertanias are there?"

"Nae mair than one, Captain, if that, but have ye been there before?"

"Certainly not. Why would we?"

"Ah well, there ye are, Captain. Ye've never been, so the ship dinna ken where Libertania might be, and I have nae idea either."

De la Beche threw up his arms in disbelief.

"I thought the systems took care of all that sort of thing, McTavish. That's your department. It should know where Libertania is, without my having to find it. Why do I bother to pay for systems when it turns out that I have to do the job myself? It really is too irksome."

"Ah seem tae remember that ye didnae pay for systems last time, Captain," came the reply, in rather acid tones.

De la Beche waved dismissively.

"Nonsense. It was payment in kind, McTavish. That little chappie – what was his name? – did the upgrade for us after we had done him a good turn. I didn't hear you complain then."

"Ye get what ye pay for, Captain. That's whit ah always say."

De la Beche shook his head.

"We all know about your sayings, McTavish. Never knowingly out-grumbled, that's you. Now, what are you going to do to get us to Libertania?"

McTavish made a sound like he was sucking air through his teeth.

"Ah'll have tae get the coordinates from *Cartographica Galactica.* It willnae be cheap."

De la Beche sighed resignedly.

"Do that, McTavish, and then get us there."

***

The *Bountiful* emerged into orbit around Planet Libertania and the crew on the Bridge stared as its image appeared on the big screen. From on high, it appeared to have a certain rather stark beauty. Three large continents, lapped by smaller seas, covered most of its surface. Wispy clouds dotted the edges of the seas, otherwise most of the land was clearly visible. Zooming in, it became apparent that much of the land was semi-desert. Only here and there, close to the land's edges, could a few patches of vegetation be seen. Even fewer were the brown and grey patchwork areas, which, on closer view, turned out to be habitations.

De la Beche stared at the screen with obvious distaste.

"Do we have any information on this benighted place, McTavish?"

McTavish materialized.

"Where in Hell are ye takin' us noo, Captain? I can find nothing aboot yon planet except a wee mention in the *Good Planet Guide.*"

De la Beche snorted and threw up his arms.

"I don't believe it. If that is so, I would like to know what their idea of a bad planet was."

"Aye. It's in the section of planets to be avoided at all costs and the entry is years oot o' date."

"Very helpful, darling. Does it actually say anything about the place?"

"The only thing I can tell ye is that the big toon is called Davy Jones and it has nothing but saloons and cat hooses. Mak of that what ye will."

De la Beche paused and thought for a few moments, and then looked around the Bridge.

"Now, darlings, before we go any further I always find that it is best to focus our minds and make sure we are all on the same page when it comes to action, because some members of this crew, naming no names and packing no drills, but you all know who I'm talking about, have a distressing habit of forgetting what they are supposed to be doing. First things first. Why do we think we are here?"

He turned to a tall, gaunt figure dressed entirely in grey.

"Mr Betelgeuse, as one of the finest minds in the Galaxy, perhaps you can enlighten us."

"We are here, Captain, to gather information which might lead us to the whereabouts of the planet Utrophia."

Jim, the cabin boy of the *Bountiful*, who had found himself in a corner of the Bridge, scrutinized the grey visage, its colour almost indistinguishable from the clothing, the eyes, nostrils and mouth only minimally defined, for signs of animation. He saw none.

"Correct, Mr Betelgeuse," said de la Beche, "and why do we want to know where said planet is?"

"Because, Captain," replied Mr Betelgeuse, "we are given to understand that a certain object, known as the Holy Kwokkah, may be secreted somewhere on the planet."

"Indeed, Mr Betelgeuse," said de la Beche, "and what is the significance of this Holy Kwokkah?"

"I believe, Captain, that it is sacred to the religious rites of the inhabitants of the planet Nullarbor, which is currently a member of the Southern Cross Federation."

"So I believe too, Mr Betelgeuse, and why is that significant?"

"Because, Captain, it appears that its whereabouts are also known to the leaders of the Orsonian Empire, who are using this knowledge in an endeavour to persuade the Nullarboreans to secede from the Southern Cross Federation and join the Orsonian Empire, thus giving them significant political and military advantage in that part of the Galaxy."

"And why is that any of our business?"

"The Southern Cross Federation has commissioned us to recover the Holy Kwokkah and prevent it falling into the hands of the Orsonian Empire."

"Which we have been endeavouring to do, Mr Betelgeuse, have we not?"

"Indeed, Captain."

Jim could not restrain a wry smile as he thought about what those endeavours were. The Trojan Horse strategy, using the Astromicans to seize the Kwokkah, which they had believed was on the Orsonian space station Arkadia, had come to a disastrous, not to say grisly, end. The only survivors were the Astromican leader, Major Schickelgrosser, and the Reverend Dreeble, one now mad, the other virtually comatose, on board the *Bountiful*.

"So now the question arises," de la Beche continued, "as to why we are here at this utterly unlovely destination. Perhaps, Sawbones, you could enlighten us."

Eyes turned to Doctor Culpepper, the ship's doctor, a thick set figure with greying hair, round face and a bulbous nose, as he took a couple of sips of his favourite whisky before answering.

"Well, Sechy, I mean Captain, I mentioned that a long time ago, when I sailed with Captain Blacksabre, a couple of his crew had claimed that they had been to the planet Utrophia, although they didn't stay long. Apparently, they met a rather hostile reception. They said they learned how to get to Utrophia when they were laying low on planet Libertania."

"Did they reveal how they managed to get there?" asked de la Beche.

"I don't think so, and even if they had, I would have forgotten. Memory not what it was, I'm afraid."

De la Beche sighed resignedly and leant back in his chair as he surveyed the company

"A very thin thread indeed, but what else have we got? Nothing else for it, I suppose. We shall have to make a little recce. From what we know this planet is stuffed full of ruffians, vagabonds and cutthroats, so types with whom we are all familiar. We need someone who could hold his own in that sort of company but is also dispensable, just in case of a little mishap."

He looked around the Bridge. Every crew member kept their head down, pretending to be preoccupied with what they were doing. Mr Betelgeuse shuffled uneasily.

"Not you, of course, Mr Betelgeuse. Let me have a think. What is Major Schickelgrosser doing now?"

"He and Reverend Dreeble are confined to quarters, Captain. You have not said what you intend to do with them."

Jim thought he detected the trace of a smile around the Captain's lips.

"I think he might be just the man for the job. I did promise the Lord High Admiral that he would never hear of the Major again, so if the worst comes to the worst, that would be one little promise kept. Now, I don't think he should go entirely alone. We need a companion to keep an eye on him."

He looked around the Bridge several times. The crew members stuck ever more intently to their tasks. Then his eye fell on Jim.

"Jim: the perfect travelling companion. No one could take exception to you. Your writing skills will come in very useful. You can go as the Major's amanuensis. Just scribble away about everything he does. None of them will be able read or write. They won't have the faintest idea what you are doing. Avoids all suspicion."

Jim stared back at the Captain, unable to say anything. He felt himself beginning to tremble and his eyes moistened.

"Oh, don't blub. It doesn't become you. With that butter-wouldn't-melt-in-your-mouth look, nothing much will happen to you unless ..." He trailed off and turned to Mr Betelgeuse. "Do they have catamites there, Mr Betelgeuse?"

"The *Good Planet Guide* makes no mention of them, Captain."

"I don't imagine it does. Somewhat *de trop* for their class of reader. Well, Jim, that might be something to watch out for, otherwise you shouldn't have much to worry about. Saddle up and prepare to go. McTavish, fetch Major Schickelgrosser.

***

Schickelgrosser appeared on the Bridge, his demeanour a little less gung-ho than Jim remembered. De la Beche gestured to him to come forward.

"Now, Major, I know you must have been terribly bored of late, but I'm glad to tell you that I have an exciting little task for you."

Schickelgrosser stiffened.

"With respect, Captain, when did you start to give me orders?"

De la Beche smiled graciously.

"Since you became our guest, darling. After your last little *debacle*, I'm afraid your stock with your previous employers is a little lower than it was. Besides, I'm sure that someone with your drive and energy wouldn't want to twiddle their thumbs forever."

Schickelgrosser grimaced, looked around the Bridge and realized he had no choice.

"OK, Captain, you win. What's the mission?"

Well, darling, it calls for drive, initiative and, ah, discretion. I'm sure you can manage at least one of those. You remember your last unfortunate encounter with the Orsonians and the quest for the Kwokkah? We have reason to believe that it may be somewhere called Utrophia. There are some who think the place is purely mythical, but I happen to think differently. We have heard that some of – shall I say – the less reputable members of the astronautical community, know it exists and, more importantly, how to get there. We are currently in the vicinity of the planet Libertania, which is the haunt of many of the said reprobates. We would like you to go there and see what you can find out. Make the acquaintance of the locals. Keep your ear to the ground. Bit of intelligence-gathering. You military types know all about that sort of thing. You can take Jim here with you. He will be your amanuensis."

"My what?"

"Your little helper, darling, your note-taker. He will keep a careful record of what happens, so you don't have to bother."

Schickelgrosser pondered, trying to work out the implications.

"Many hostiles there?"

"Well, in the nature of their, ah, calling, they are not always the most welcoming of individuals, but someone of your charm and amiability should be able to manage."

Schickelgrosser nodded.

"Mission accepted, Captain."

"Excellent. The best of luck to you both. Helmsman, prepare the cutter."

2

The cutter deposited Schickelgrosser and Jim a short distance outside the town of Davy Jones. The ramp descended and Schickelgrosser bounded down, weapon in hand, and crouched defensively, pointing the weapon outwards and scanning the horizon for threats. He swivelled ninety degrees clockwise three times, each time making sure no enemy was in sight. He then motioned silently for Jim to join him and bring their packs. The cutter pilot viewed their actions with evident amusement, gave them a cheery wave as they walked away, and sped off back to the *Bountiful*.

"You got your weapon, soldier?"

Jim nodded. He omitted to tell the Major that he had no idea how to use it. They walked along a dirt road towards the town. The heat and humidity made it feel as if they were wading through treacle, all the time fending off fierce, biting flies. At the town's edge they saw a large billboard:

The *Dead Mans Chest*
Davy Jones'Finest Saloon
Debauchery Guaranteed
You will not be disappointed

The Major read the sign with evident appreciation.

"I think we'll just mosey on down there, soldier. I fancy getting myself some real whiskey. I don't much care for that Shampain and winey-wine they drink on that spaceship."

They reached the outskirts of the town and turned a corner into what seemed to be the main street, off which ran numerous narrow alleys. The road was paved with rough stone and full of potholes. A very few, battered vehicles could be seen, none of them moving. The buildings were mostly low, ramshackle and made of brick or wood. Many seemed to be saloons or joints offering other delights, often with scantily-dressed females attempting to entice passers-by into entering. Jim found himself fascinated.

"Eyes ahead, soldier," said Schickelgrosser, sternly.

At a crossroads, they came across a building larger than most, sporting a billboard featuring a massively-endowed female figure dressed in leather jumpsuit and thigh-length boots. Underneath the picture it read:

The Courthouse
Her Honor Judge Malignia Maleficia
Libertania's Strictest Judge
Justice As You Need It – Hot and Strong and Severe
Hanging and Flaying a Speciality

They both stared at the billboard for a few moments before Schickelgrosser grunted and pushed Jim forward. As they walked, a few figures were visible, most sitting idly on benches by the side of the road, taking little notice of anything around them, not even of what appeared to be a drunk, bottle in hand, lying on the ground, yelling and kicking out at a pack of huge rats that were attacking him. Schickelgrosser pulled out his weapon and fired twice. Two rats exploded in a cloud of fur and gore. The rest of the pack scurried off, yelping. Schickelgrosser ran over and pulled the drunk to his feet.

"You alright, soldier? I just saved your ass."

The drunk gazed wide-eyed at the apparition before him, with its wide-brimmed hat, shades and battle fatigues, leaned forward and vomited over him. Schickelgrosser yelled "Sonofabitch!" and cracked the drunk across the face. He fell to the ground and lay there, to catcalls from some of the figures on the benches. Schickelgrosser glared back at them. They fell silent. He looked across the road and pointed Jim to a large sign on the building opposite which read "The *Dead Man's Chest.*"

"OK soldier, let's leave this asshole and get ourselves a drink."

They went inside to a lobby. A large sign read "All weapons to be left here"; another announced "Gold, silver or cash money only. All types accepted." There was a ringing noise, clearly an alarm, and a metallic voice intoned, "Weapons detected. Weapons detected. Please lodge them with the attendant." In a corner of the lobby, they saw the attendant looking at them expectantly from behind a counter.

"Your weapons please, gents."

Schickelgrosser demurred, but the attendant was insistent.

"House rules, gents. No one gets in with a weapon."

Schickelgrosser shrugged and nodded to Jim. The attendant eyed the two blasters they put on the counter with evident appreciation.

"Haven't seen one of these before. You boys new around here?"

"Yeah. We're from out of town. Been working hard lately. Come here for a bit of rest and recreation."

The attendant smiled knowingly.

"You've come to the right place, gents. You can get everything you could ever think of here, and a lot more besides. Just go on in and take your pleasure."

Inside, the bar was large, dark and cavernous. The walls were lined with portraits of males in what looked like fancy dress and what Jim recognized as ancient weapons – swords, daggers, pikes and such. Smoke from a great many cheroots and hookahs filled the air, so that they could not see where it ended. It was busy, though not crowded, with individuals of every race and type, dressed in an extraordinary collection of apparel. Some wore large double-breasted jackets, others pantaloons and boots. Many affected bandanas and other headgear. All were clothed in bright colours. Lightly-clad females, equally diverse in appearance, walked round serving drinks or draping themselves around semi-comatose customers. No one seemed to take much notice of them.

Schickelgrosser looked down at his vomit-stained tunic. "I gotta get cleaned up." He went over to the bar and beckoned to the barman.

"You got somewhere I can wipe this off? Drunken son of a bitch outside damn puked all over me."

The barman looked quizzical.

"Rosco? Why, what did you do to him?"

Schickelgrosser grew enraged.

"Do to him? Why I saved his damn ass, that's what I did to him. He was damn near being eaten by rats. I got a couple of them and the rest skeedaddled."

The barman shook his head.

"You didn't want to do that. They're his friends."

"Friends! Whaddya mean friends?"

"He gets rat-arsed in here and then he goes outside and the rats get his arse. They only nibble. He gets off on it. It's the only way he can get it up."

Schickelgrosser snorted derisively.

"What kind of place is this! I need a drink. Gimme a bottle of your best whiskey and something for soldier Jim, here. Where's the rest room, so I can clean up?"

Jim sat down at a table and tried his drink. It was quite pleasant, slightly sweet with a flowery aroma. Several minutes later, Schickelgrosser returned, a large damp patch on his tunic and trousers where the vomit had been. He sat down, took several large slugs of whiskey and then looked around.

"Take a look, soldier. Low lifes and hussies, wall to wall. Give me a few men and I'd soon be having them tell me everything they know." He looked at Jim and shook his head. "We're gonna have to play our cards different."

Just then, one of the females came over to them. She was brown-skinned, curvaceous, with dark, lustrous hair and dressed in an almost diaphanous shift. She had a smile that was both friendly and alluring. Jim was struck almost dumb.

"What have we here? Where did you two come from?"

The voice was warm, velvety, sensuous.

Schickelgrosser rose quickly from his chair.

"Well howdy, Ma'am. We're from out of town. Just got here."

She laughed

"More from out of this world, if you ask me!"

Schickelgrosser allowed himself a little smile and indicated a chair.

"Kind of, Ma'am. Won't you join us?"

She smiled, eased herself into the chair and turned to Jim.

"And who is this?"

"That's Jim, Ma'am, my, ah ... my little helper."

She ran her fingers down Jim's cheek, then down his body to the top of his thigh.

"So young, so sweet and so helpful, I'm sure."

Jim found himself unable to move or to say anything. She turned back to the Major.

"And what do you do?"

"I'm a soldier, Ma'am."

Her eyes widened and a slight shiver ran down her body.

"Oh, a soldier. I do love a soldier. So strong, so manly. And do you kill?"

Schickelgrosser straightened in his chair and his chest puffed up.

"Yes, Ma'am. That's what soldiers do."

"Oh, I know. It gives me goose bumps just to think of it. You must be very brave."

Her fingers gently caressed Schickelgrosser's neck and then began to move down his chest.

"I guess so, Ma'am. If you're a soldier, you're either brave or you're dead. No other way."

She undid the top button of his tunic and slid her hand inside.

"I can feel you're so, so very much alive, you must be very, very brave. Have you killed many?"

"Plenty, Ma'am. I didn't stop to count 'em."

Jim stared fascinated at the shape of her hand under the tunic, moving rhythmically across Schickelgrosser's pectorals.

"Do tell me, how do you kill them?"

Jim saw that Schickelgrosser's posture was stiffening and his breathing becoming deeper.

"Every which way, Ma'am – weapons, force fields, hand-to-hand."

Her eyes widened. She moved her head closer and undid several more buttons as her hand slid down over his stomach and toyed with his belt.

"Oh, hand-to-hand. I want to know more about hand-to-hand. Tell me all about hand-to-hand."

He took a couple of deep breaths.

"Well, Ma'am, if you want to kill in hand-to-hand combat you really need a knife – and if he has a knife, then you need to know about knife-fighting. Let me show you."

He rose from the chair and took up a semi-crouching stance, head down, with one arm bent in front of his chin.

"First, you have to have the right stand – one foot forward, free hand guarding the throat so he can't slash it. You've got to be aggressive, always moving forward, don't give him time to think. Now there are six ways you can launch a knife attack. You can come straight down on him – we call that a vertical attack – you can make a forward diagonal attack, a reverse diagonal attack, a forward horizontal strike, a reverse horizontal strike or a forward thrust. They're all good. It just depends on how he comes at you.

Then you need to know what to go for. Slash across the throat or stab to the heart, if you want to kill; groin and top of the leg, if you just want to get him down."

His knife arm made slashing arcs and thrusts to demonstrate. As he moved, she uttered little squeaks of admiration. When he sat down, she put her head very near his. One hand rubbed the back of his neck, the other moved ever lower down his stomach.

"Oh, don't stop. You are making me so very, very excited. Let's go somewhere private. I want you to tell me about every thrust and parry. I want to know about all the blood and the guts and the screams."

Shickelgrosser gave a smile, which turned into a smirk, and winked at Jim.

"You stay here for a while, Jim boy, while I tell this young lady all about how we soldiers do our fighting."

She gave another little squeak and took him by the hand. Jim watched as they disappeared from view through an opening that he could dimly make out at the far end of the bar.

Jim sat back on his seat, nursing his drink. Half an hour went by, and then an hour. He wasn't certain how long these things were supposed to take. In fact, he wasn't certain what exactly the things were. He could only guess, but after two hours he felt that maybe he should make some enquiries. He went to the bar and called the barman over.

"I wonder if you can help me? My friend went through that door at the end of the bar a couple of hours ago and he hasn't come back. Do you know where he might have gone?"

The barman looked him up and down.

"Your friend? D'you mean the old guy that Rosco puked over?"

In the circumstances, Jim thought that was as good a description as any other.

"Yes, that's him."

"Did he go with anyone?"

"Yes, a young lady."

The barman looked at Jim for a couple of seconds, pursing his lips.

"Dark hair, a looker, dressed all pretty, talking even prettier?"

Jim was beginning to admire the barman's talent for pithy descriptions.

"Yes, that sounds like her."

The barman gave a half-smile and shook his head.

"That's Circe. If your friend went with her, you can forget about him. You won't see him again."

Jim recoiled, astonished and alarmed.

"What do you mean, I won't see him again? What's happened to him?"

The barman opened his arms and shrugged.

"I'm not going to tell you, and you don't want to know. Take my advice, Sonny, and leave while you can. This is no place for you."

The barman moved off down the bar to serve another customer. Jim stood transfixed, wondering what to do next. Eventually, he decided he had best take the barman's advice. The place clearly had unknown dangers. He was suddenly glad for Schickelgrosser's insistence that he bring a weapon, even if he wasn't sure how to use it. He went to the entrance lobby to collect it. The figure at the desk looked at him quizzically.

"No record. When did you say you brought it in?"

"About two and a half hours ago. I came in with my friend, an older gentleman, a soldier. We both handed our weapons in."

The desk clerk tapped a screen and shook his head.

"Nope, nothing here."

Jim was becoming exasperated.

"Look, I'm absolutely certain. It was only a couple of hours ago. Can you check again?"

More shaking of the head.

"Screen says no, so no it is. Besides, Kid, you don't look old enough to handle a piece. I probably couldn't give it back to you even if I had it."

Jim stared at the clerk but all he saw was an expression of faintly amused disparagement. What they said about Libertania was true. Thievery was the norm. The attendant had taken a fancy to the weapon and knew that there was nothing Jim could do about it. He was not going to get his weapon back and he realized that his position was becoming perilous. He had better try to get help.

He still had his communicator, but he could not risk anyone seeing him using it, so he went outside.

As he came out, he saw the figure of Rosco across the street, this time standing upright, with several rats around him. Rosco caught sight of him and started yelling. Jim, alarmed, began to run. He glanced backwards and saw Rosco and the rats running after him and catching up fast. There was nothing for it. He had to get off the street. He lunged at the nearest door, which swung open as he hit it and he fell, head first, down some steps, sprawling over the floor.

For a few seconds, he was too stunned to react. Then his vision cleared and still face down he saw a large boot, alongside which dangled several leather thongs. He forced himself to look up; his eyes travelled over boots that extended to the thigh, over leather-clad belly and mountainous breasts to a stern-jawed face surrounded by long, blond hair. He heard a deep, though clearly female, voice.

"What have we here?"

3

Sometimes, thought Commander Splenditheran, all the benefits and privileges of his exalted position as Supreme Leader of the Ruling Council of the Southern Cross Federation were not enough to compensate for some of the irksome duties he was called upon to perform. The current duty was irksome in the extreme. Why, he mused, did I imagine that any theological question could ever be resolved? Then, after a few more moments' reflection, why did I not remember that any attempt to resolve a theological question always made things worse?

He was sitting in his place in the chair of the Ruling Council Chamber. Alongside him were senior members of the Council and across from them were the High Sapient of the Non-Inflationary Denomination of the Sacrosanctity of Reason and the High Priest of the planet Nullarbor. He had hoped that the two divines would find some sort of understanding. After all, they each claimed to believe in a benign higher authority. That, in turn, he hoped would help soothe the concerns of the Nullarboreans, who were once again threatening to leave the Federation, after he had informed them that the Kwokkah had not yet been recovered. He shuddered to think what they might do if they ever found out about the debacle with the Astromicans.

Instead of reaching understanding, discussion between them rapidly became as rancorous as it was incomprehensible. What seemed to be arcane points in metaphysics were bandied about with ferocious intensity. Splenditheran decided he had better intervene before things became completely out of hand.

"Please forgive my intervention, but those of us on this side of the table are not as well versed in these matters as you are and so, perhaps for our benefit, you could explain, in simpler terms, what you are discussing and perhaps we could help to arrive at a conclusion that we could all agree on. If you would like to start, Your Most Cerebral Intelligence," he said to the High Sapient. Turning to the High Priest, he suggested "and then you could respond, Your Sublime Righteousness."

There was silence before the High Sapient replied.

"We were discussing what happens to the spirit, or, as we would prefer, the essence, of those who have passed on, but had not given themselves to right living. We both agree that they are cast into an abyss. In our case, we believe that abyss is a black hole that we call *ultima cava*. Where we differ is what happens after that. I have pointed out that the laws of physics, bequeathed to us by the Supreme Ineffability, do not allow information to be destroyed. Consequently, the essence of those departed remains trapped on the surface of *ultima cava*, at the event horizon. Furthermore, the laws of physics also show that all black holes emit radiation, so that the essence of those trapped is gradually returned to the Universe. That explains the continued existence of evil and wrongdoing."

The High Priest, a portly, bearded figure wearing a red turban and brown full-length robe, shook his head vigorously.

"In the Apophthegms of the Prophet Goannah, all blessings to him, it is written, 'The spirits of the damned will be cast into eternal Fire and they will long to leave the Fire, but never will they leave the Fire and their's will be an everlasting torment.'"

The High Sapient became agitated again.

"That is entirely unreasonable. Why would the Supreme Ineffability give us the laws of physics and then deliberately violate them?"

The ire of the High Priest was also rising.

"It is written that there is only one law, the law of Koalah. Koalah gives and Koalah takes away. Blessed be His name."

Splenditheran had had enough. He decided to cut things short.

"Thank you, Your Most Cerebral Intelligence, and you, Your Sublime Righteousness, for a most rewarding discussion. I can't begin to say how much it has enlightened us. Now if you will forgive us, we have some rather boring Council business to conduct." He gestured and a flunkey appeared. "No doubt you would like to continue your discussion over dinner?"

Splenditheran allowed himself a sigh of relief as he watched them disappear through the Chamber exit, still arguing. He turned to the other members of the Council.

"What should we make of that, Councillors?"

The Chief of Staff was first to respond.

"They're both full of shit."

Splenditheran saw the Secretary of Finance, a rather prissy individual, given to making long-winded, nit-picking points, wince.

"I must protest, Mister Chairman. The High Sapient is a most learned person, someone of the highest integrity, and a true devotee of the Supreme Ineffability. He should not be spoken of in those terms."

Splenditheran paused. He rather agreed with the Chief of Staff, but obviously could not say so. Besides, the Chief of Staff had been getting above himself lately. He needed to be taken down a peg or two.

"I quite agree, Mister Secretary. That was no way to refer to our most revered prelate. You must be a little more respectful, Chief of Staff."

The Chief of Staff grimaced but said nothing. Splenditheran continued.

"The situation on Nullarbor is becoming very dangerous. The Kwokkah business has unsettled them completely. The Orsonians have been up to their usual tricks. They have been paying religious fanatics to stir up all sorts of trouble while offering inducements to the religious establishment to come over to them. Our security services report that the situation is on a knife-edge. They could defect at any moment. The Kwokkah is the key. If we can recover it, then I think the Nullarboreans can be persuaded to stay with us."

There was silence while the Council digested the news. Then the Chief of Staff spoke.

"I say the Nullarboreans are full of shit."

The Chief of Staff was a military type. Splenditheran had long known that all military types judged all non-military types by degrees of ordure. The Chief of Staff pressed on.

"Why do we need that bunch of towelheads? I say we kick them out. The Orsonians are welcome to them."

Splenditheran had trouble containing his astonishment.

"I am astonished at you, Chief of Staff. That would leave that part of our frontier very vulnerable."

The Chief of Staff shook his head dismissively.

"Don't really think so. There are a few planets around there that the Orsonians might take but, frankly, we wouldn't miss them. More trouble than they're worth, in my opinion. While they are cock-a-hoop about snaffling a few trifles, we need to look at the big picture and stop worrying about itsy-bitsy stuff."

This time, Splenditheran didn't bother to contain his astonishment.

"You astound me, Chief of Staff. What exactly do you mean by 'the big picture'?"

"I say we go for it. Make a big move."

"Go for what? Move where?"

A faint smile appeared on the Chief of Staff's face.

"Well, let's start with the Arcturans."

A collective gasp went up from the rest of the Council.

"Are you seriously suggesting that we invade the Arcturan Empire?" asked Splenditheran.

The Chief of Staff nodded.

"Why not? They're there for the taking. It would be a piece of cake."

Splenditheran had to sit back and compose himself before replying.

"Have you taken leave of your senses, Chief of Staff? What do you imagine the reaction would be in the rest of the Galaxy? That could start a general Galactic war."

The Chief of Staff gave a dismissive snort.

"I don't think so. Not if we're quick. There wouldn't be any resistance. The Arcturans are all drug-addled layabouts, only interested in having a good time. They wouldn't know what hit them if we go for it. We take them and we would be sitting pretty – the biggest thing in the Galaxy. No one else could touch us. There would be the usual moans and groans, but all the rest of them would just have to suck it up."

Splenditheran stared hard at the Chief of Staff, trying to gauge whether he was really serious. He could not be absolutely sure, but in any event, it was time to put a stop to this nonsense.

"I think we can all agree that there is no question of our taking action of that sort. The consequences would be catastrophic."

He looked around. All the other members of the Council, except the Chief of Staff, nodded their assent.

4

Jim tried to think of something to say, but realized the impossibility of explaining his situation. All that came out was a sort of moan.

"It's not the way clients normally come for business, dearie. They don't usually start on themselves before I get to work on them, but we take all comers."

She placed her boot on Jim's neck and lightly wafted the thongs of the whip she held over his face.

"Now, what would you like me to send you down for?"

Fear was beginning to turn to panic. Jim looked around and saw he was in a darkened room. In the gloom he could make out what appeared to be an iron bedstead, with various straps and manacles hanging from it. On the wall, dangling from racks, were whips, cudgels, straps and other implements clearly designed to inflict pain. In one corner he could see an iron cage, in another a chair. He moaned again.

"Refusing to plead, I see. Then I shall have to pronounce sentence. As this is the first time you have been before me, I shall be lenient. Fifty lashes and then a ten-stretch." She pointed to a large wheel. "It gives the most exquisite pain. You will absolutely revel in it."

Panic was now all Jim felt.

"Please, no! I didn't mean to come in here. Please let me go."

She stiffened, and then cracked the whip.

"Silence in court! I am Her Honor Judge Malignia. If you have anything to say, you address me as Your Honor. Is that understood?"

Jim just managed to get out the words.

"Yes, Your Honor."

"Hmph. Any more of this and I shall sentence you to the Electric Chair. I reserve that punishment for the most incorrigible prisoners."

She clicked her fingers. Jim saw emerge from the gloom a crooked figure with a distinct limp.

"Bruno, prepare the chair."

"Yeth, Your Honor."

He shambled over to the chair in the corner and touched the wall. Immediately, the chair lit up and emitted several sparks.

"You have been warned. Contempt of Court is a most serious offence. Now, before we start, you must pay the fine."

Jim almost forgot his fear, in his bemusement.

"The fine?"

She cracked the whip again

"Yes, the fine. You pay the fine and then I administer your punishment. That's how it works. You have money with you, I take it, otherwise why would you come here?"

The fear returned. On Libertania, they only dealt with physical money like cash. Schickelgrosser had been put in charge of the purse. Jim had no money on him. He didn't think he had much option but to ask for mercy.

"I don't have any money. Please don't punish me. I really didn't mean to come in here. I was trying to escape from Rosco and his rats."

She snorted.

"Rosco's harmless, and so are his rats. Why would you be escaping from him?" Jim realized that he was in even deeper trouble. For a few moments he thought it might be best to keep quiet and take his punishment, but the fear of pain was too great.

"Well, you see, I came to Libertania with another gentlemen, who, er, isn't here at the moment, and we came from a spaceship ..."

"A spaceship?"

"Yes, a spaceship. HMS *Bountiful.*"

"HMS *Bountiful*?"

"Yes, HMS *Bountiful*. It's a privateer."

Her Honor Madame Malignia shook her head.

"A privateer. Whatever next? Young man, you have the most vivid imagination. I don't believe a word you say. Bruno, frisk him. Let's see if he really doesn't have any money?"

Jim froze as he felt Bruno's clammy hand feel all over his body and delve into his pockets. Bruno pulled out the communicator and held it up.

"No money, Your Honor, only thith."

Her Honor waved dismissively.

"Put it on the table. Now, prepare the cage."

Bruno shuffled over to the iron cage in the corner of the room, took a large key from his belt and after a bout of fiddling, the door swung open.

"Ith ready, Your Honor."

She cracked the whip twice at Jim.

"In you get."

For a moment Jim thought he might make a run for it but his body was almost paralyzed with fear. He felt tears begin to well up.

"Why do I have to get in?"

Her Honor cracked the whip again.

"Because I say so. No money means you have to earn your keep. You will be my personal submissive. I shall punish you most severely and you will be most grateful. Is that understood?"

Jim didn't understand at all. He thought desperately of something to say, but nothing came. Then he felt Bruno's hand on his shoulder and he was dragged across the room and thrust inside, as the door clanged behind him.

Her Honor looked sternly at him and then, without a word, aimed a kick at Bruno, who yelped as the sharp toe of her boot hit his buttock. She then marched through a door at the far end of the room.

Jim sat slumped in the cage, quite unable to believe what had happened to him. Despair rose, as he began to think he might never get out. He closed his eyes and began to cry.

Hours passed, and, while his sobs had subsided, he could see no prospect of escape. Deep despair was beginning to set in, when he heard Bruno making what sounded like clucking noises. He opened his eyes and saw him jabbing a finger at the communicator, which was still on the table and flashing as he touched it. Bruno turned around to look at him.

"I like thith. How do you play?"

For a second, Jim thought of refusing to answer. Then he had an idea..

"Bring it over here, and I'll show you."

Bruno hesitated, then picked it up and came over to the cage. Jim motioned him to hold it through the bars and made some gestures across its screen. Immediately pictures appeared and music began playing. Bruno clucked in delight.

"I like it. I like it."

They both listened as Bruno swayed in time to the music. Then he showed pictures and animation that delighted Bruno even more. After a while, Jim asked, "Would you like it to talk to you?"

Bruno looked astonished.

"It talk to me?"

"Yes, of course. Look, I'll show you."

He tried to call the *Bountiful*. It took a while. Maybe there were technical problems or, more likely, Jim thought, the *Bountiful*'s signals operator, Gobby ("Gobby by name, Gobby by nature"), was drunk.

Eventually, after numerous buzzes and whistles, a voice that he recognized as Gobby's answered, relatively uninebriated. Before Gobby had time to say much, Jim spoke.

"Gobby, I'm here with my friend Bruno. Will you say hello to him."

After a moment's hesitation, the answer came, a hint of puzzlement in the voice.

"Hello, Bruno."

Bruno, delighted, danced a little jig.

"It talkth to me. It talkth to me."

While Bruno was distracted, Jim tried to tell Gobby what had happened, but the words tumbled out so fast and so randomly that they made little sense. Eventually he managed to convey to Gobby that Schickelgrosser had disappeared, maybe kidnapped, and he, Jim, was in trouble. Gobby tutted, rather superciliously.

"Blimey, Jim, you've got yourself into a right old barney. I'd better tell the Captain. I expect he'll want to give you a good bollocking."

Jim thought that was uncalled for. He waited in trepidation for what seemed ages, until he heard the languid tones of de la Beche.

"Jim, darling, I understand you are with someone called Bruno, to whom I am supposed to say hello. Is that correct?"

"Yes, he's here."

"Well hello there, Bruno. How are you?"

Bruno gazed at the communicator in wonderment.

"I'th very well, thank you."

"Very glad to hear it, Bruno darling. I understand that you have been entertaining young Jim. You won't mind if I have a word with him, will you?"

Bruno gave a grunt that de la Beche took to be affirmative.

"I hear that you have got yourself into something of a pickle, Jim. Do tell all. I've been feeling rather bored, so I'm hoping to hear something to amuse me."

Jim retold the saga, this time a little more coherently. As he finished, he heard the sound of a sigh come over the airwaves.

"The Major is very accident-prone, isn't he? Twice is beginning to look like carelessness, as someone once remarked. And now you say you are in a cage and are no doubt hoping for rescue. What to do? What to do? Let me think."

Jim waited again as the communicator went silent. Then de la Beche's voice returned, rather crisper this time.

"Nothing else for it. I see we have the coordinates of that establishment. We'll have to come down and see for ourselves."

5

The Lord High Admiral of the Orsonian Battle Fleet looked into the mirror, feeling even more satisfied with himself than usual. Giving only a cursory glance at the pictures of wives, mistresses and children that adorned his office, he turned to the matter in hand. Reports from the planet Nullarbor indicated that attempts to induce the Nullarboreans to join the Empire were making progress. Final success was only a matter of time.

It had taken a lot of effort. Large inducements had to be offered to various Nullarborean religious leaders. As always, the more devout and revered the divine, the more expensive they were. The amount demanded by the High Priest was so extortionate that the Admiral had balked at paying it. Worse, the High Priest had also demanded sight of the Kwokkah, or at the very least incontrovertible proof that the Orsonians had it.

The Admiral was confident that he would succeed without help from the High Priest, who would be given very short shrift once Nullarbor was within the empire. However, as an insurance policy, he had summoned the Superior Archimandrite of the Holy Synodrin, who had now been ushered in. The Archimandrite had a reputation for being unsurpassed in obsequiousness among the Orsonian hierarchy and had a predeliction for elaborate rituals, gorgeously-embroidered vestments, the finest wines and little boys. He bowed low on entering.

"All peace and blessings of Zoabh be upon you, my Lord. May He guide you in all your deeds and sanctify your righteous acts."

Before answering, the Admiral made a mental note to require a similar sycophantic attitude from the other prelates who aspired to the top job of Supreme Hierophant of the Holy Synodrin. The current incumbent was becoming too full of himself. He had even begun to claim divine inspiration for his actions, so clearly needed replacing. He returned the bow with a cursory nod.

"And all blessings to you too, Your Sincerity. Now, I have a very special request to make. It is a task only someone of your standing and sanctity could undertake."

The Archimandrite bowed low again.

"As ever, my Lord, my prayers are at your command."

"I am most grateful, Your Sincerity. I have some good news. We hope very soon to welcome the planet Nullarbor into the Empire." The Admiral ignored the faint frown that flickered across the face of the Archimandrite. "To mark the occasion, we intend to restore to them their most sacred object, the Holy Kwokkah, which we understand is somewhere on the holy planet Utrophia. Now, as you know, I and all others who are not members of religious orders are forbidden from communicating with Utrophia, but you, of course, are not. So I hope you will assist me in this most important task."

Conflicting emotions seemed to struggle for control of the Archimandrite's expression. Eventually, he managed to reply.

"Of course, I will do what I can to assist you, My Lord, but could I just remind you that the Nullarboreans are followers of the false prophet Goannah and that, according to our holy scriptural accounts, the Kwokkah is a fabrication, created by the mad monk Galab."

The Admiral made light of any objections.

"Oh, I know those of you of godly inclinations have your little differences, but I'm sure you can work things out. After all, we all believe in more or less the same thing, don't we?"

The Archimandrite had barely begun to reply, "Well … ," before the Admiral interjected.

"That's settled, then. Let me know how you get on."

The Archimandrite bowed low once more and slowly left, head bowed as if deep in contemplation.

As he watched him depart, the Admiral decided he had no time to lose.

"Civil Servant 21346, please ask the Vice Admiral to come and see me."

As was the Orsonian custom, the Admiral loathed any and all of his immediate underlings, regarding them as shifty and untrustworthy and suspecting them of perpetually scheming to replace him. As a consequence, the Vice Admiral needed to be brought into every plan of action, so that he could not feign ignorance and escape his share of any blame if anything went wrong.

The Vice Admiral was shown in; the Admiral ordered Civil Servant 21346 to stay and take notes. He began by pointing to a map of the near Galaxy on a large screen.

"With Nullarbor in the bag, we can take these others." He indicated several nearby planets. "Those Southern Cross boobies will be crying their eyes out, but they won't be able to do anything about it. The question is, what else might they do?"

The Vice Admiral leaned back in his chair.

"I think they'll try to take the neutral zone, Lord High Admiral. If they didn't, it would leave them very vulnerable."

The Admiral nodded.

"Exactly what I was thinking. So we would need to move first. We take the neutral zone and then we have the Southern Cross exactly where we want them. No more nonsense from them from now on."

The Vice Admiral broke into a broad smile. For once, he thought, the High Admiral proposed doing something he agreed with.

"An excellent strategy, Lord High Admiral." Then he hesitated. "There might be one problem, though. What about the Feminarchs?"

The Admiral laughed derisively.

"What could that bunch of harpies do against our mighty battle fleet? Getting rid of them once and for all would be the biggest benefit of the whole operation. For too long, they have been poisoning the minds of females all over the Galaxy. I know our females are far too sensible and virtuous to take any notice of them, but I have heard tales from other rulers of the appalling damage that their wicked ideas have done. They need to be exterminated. We will show them no mercy."

He turned to the civil servant.

"Civil Servant 21346, I want you to draw up headings for an Action Plan. There will be a need for treaties with Nullarbor and any other planets that we annex, and then we must start forming a Battle Plan for an invasion of the neutral zone and for dealing with our inevitable victory. There should be standard plans for most of that on file. Is that clear?"

"Most of it is clear, Lord High Admiral. There is just one question. You mentioned 'show no mercy' when dealing with the Feminarchs. What exactly does that mean?"

Was this Civil Servant 21346 up to his usual tricks? The Admiral couldn't be bothered wasting time finding out.

"I would have thought that was obvious."

Civil Servant 21346 contemplated with dismay the notion of all those females going to waste, when on Orson all females were monopolized by the great and powerful like the Admiral.

"That might be against the Galactic Conventions on Warfare, Lord High Admiral."

The Admiral realized that Civil Servant 21346 *was* up to his usual tricks. He needed to be put in his place.

"These are *females*, Civil Servant 21346. What do the Galactic Conventions have to say about *females*?"

The civil servant was taken aback. He had no idea.

"I'm not quite sure, Lord High Admiral. I will have to check. From memory, I don't believe the Conventions mention the gender of prisoners of war."

"Exactly," said the Admiral, a note of triumph in his voice. "The Galactic Conventions only apply to civilized society and no civilized society allows females in combat. Therefore the Conventions do not apply in this case. If they were males it would be different, but since they are females, we can do as we see fit. Get on with your work, Civil Servant 21346."

As Civil Servant 21346 left, the Admiral turned to his deputy.

"I think this is just the start of something much bigger."

"Like what?"

"Like the Arcturans."

A look of surprise on the Vice Admiral's face was quickly followed by a broad grin.

"Tricky ... but possible."

6

Jim had drifted off to sleep in his cage when he was awakened by a sharp rap. He saw Bruno shamble over to open the front door and, framed in the door, appeared de la Beche, wearing his Libertania outfit – flared cerise pantaloons gathered at the ankles over heavy, studded boots and an emerald ruched blouse under a cutaway camouflage jacket. On his head was a crimson turban and a gold and diamond pendant. He gazed down at Bruno.

"Can you tell me who is in charge here, darling?"

Bruno grimaced and grunted. Jim saw the door at the back of the room open; Her Honor entered. Whip in hand, she marched up to the front door and looked de la Beche in the eye.

"*I* am in charge. What is it that you want?"

De la Beche smiled.

"I can see you are, darling. I am Captain Sir Sechaverell de la Beche, *bart*, master of HMS *Bountiful*. Since we are meeting formally, you may address me as Sir Sechaverell. To whom do I have the honour of speaking?"

Jim saw that she stiffened slightly before replying.

"I am Her Honor, Judge Malignia Maleficia, the senior Judge of this establishment. You may address me as Your Honor."

De la Beche gave a bow as he gazed at her outfit, his eyes lingering over the layers of leather studded with brass and iron and the claws dangling from each breast.

"Delighted to make your acquaintance, Your Honor, and, if I may, can I compliment you on your attire? So becoming for a member of the judiciary."

Jim thought he saw Her Honor relax a little.

"And if I may say so, Sir Sechaverell, can I compliment you on *your* wardrobe? So smart and tasteful, unlike the slovenliness you see so much of in this town. Won't you please come in?"

De la Beche stepped into the room. Jim held his breath, hoping to catch his eye, but the Captain did not seem to glance towards the cage.

"Now, Your Honor, if I may come to the point, I understand that a member of my crew, Jim, the cabin boy, is currently enjoying your hospitality. We are, of course, grateful for your looking after him, but I am afraid we do need him back with us. Duties and all that. I'm sure you understand."

Her Honor gave a sigh.

"I'm not sure about that, Sir Sechaverell. I had some ideas for duties that he could perform for me. It's so difficult to get anyone to do things these days, as I'm sure you understand. I really don't want to let him go, but let's not fall out. Would you like to take tea with me?"

"Delighted, Your Honor."

She motioned him to sit down at a small table and snapped her fingers.

"Bruno, tea for two and some music."

"Yeth, Your Honor."

"It's Lord Pakenham, a rather spicy blend that I'm particularly fond of. I hope it will be to your taste?"

"Absolutely, one of my favourites."

De la Beche watched Bruno disappear through the door.

"I see you have a hunchback. How very clever of you. They're so hard to find these days. They're usually snapped up as soon as they appear. And yours is so perfect – the limp and the lisp, to say nothing of all those warts on his face. The one on the nose – so big and hairy. I don't think I've ever seen finer."

Jim had the impression that the beginnings of a smile appeared on Her Honor's face.

"Yes, Bruno is a treasure. I'm very fond of him. He's been with me a long time."

Just then, Jim heard strains of music and saw de la Beche cock his head to one side.

"If I'm not mistaken, Your Honor, I do believe that's *Liascia A'mor* from Handel's *Orlando*?"

Her Honor, visibly surprised, sat back in her chair.

"You astonish me, Sir Sechaverell! I never expected to meet a person of such sensitivity and refinement in this benighted part of the Galaxy. You are quite right. I have a particular passion for Handel. I often pronounce sentence to *Dal crudel che m'ha traditato* from *Tamerlano*. The sense of impending fate adds piquancy to the punishment."

De la Beche clapped his hands and beamed.

"We share a passion, Your Honor. George Frideric is simply the finest composer who ever lived. I will let you in to a little secret. I am hoping to complete his unfinished opera, *Oedipus Rex*. I'm sure you know the story. I already have a couple of motifs and a most delightful saraband. It's sure to take the musical world by storm."

Her Honor let out a gasp of admiration.

"I'm sure it will, Sir Sechaverell, and I hope I will be able to see it."

"Of course, Your Honor. I will make sure that your name is at the top of the guest list for the premiere."

They sat in silence for a while, listening to the music. Then de la Beche spoke.

"Much as this is a great pleasure, Your Honor, I must be getting along. I do hope you will let young Jim come with me. We have some rather important business to attend to."

Her Honor took several seconds to reply.

"Well, Sir Sechaverell, I find it impossible to refuse a person of your sensibility. Such a delight to meet someone who appreciates the finest things in life." She snapped her fingers. "Bruno, fetch the boy."

Jim appeared before them, blinking and stiff. De la Beche gave him a friendly smile.

"Now, Jim, I know you will want to thank Her Honor – and, of course, Bruno – for their hospitality and the way they have looked after you. Who knows what might have happened to you if they hadn't taken you in?"

Jim blinked several times and gulped before he could reply.

"Thank you for having me."

Her Honor nodded graciously.

"You are always welcome, Jim. Come back any time."

7

"It's not looking good." Junipa stared gloomily at her communicator as she and Orestia watched the incoming messages. "I never cease to be amazed at how males can whip up hysteria over nonexistent entities and their absurd demands to be worshipped and obeyed. Those Nullarborean males are particularly appalling."

She glanced up at the painting by Gentiligia Artimesci of Egregia and her maid stealing out from the chamber of the Thragian general Drakoles with his severed head in a basket. It gave her only a little comfort.

"I presume it's all about this Kwokkah thing, whatever it might be. Do you think the Orsonians are behind it?" asked Orestia. "If they go over to the Orsonians, we would have real trouble."

Junipa gave a shrug. "Probably they are stirring things, but the Nullarboreans don't need much help to work themselves up into a frenzy over anything, particularly something supposedly sacred."

"What can we do? How many members do we have there?"

"Not as many as we would like, and they are keeping their heads down right now. You know what females there have to suffer – wrapped head to toe in the drabbest clothes, not allowed education, kept in domestic slavery and continually impregnated. It's a wonder we have any members there at all."

The messages kept coming; it was evident that testosterone levels were beginning to rise all over the Galaxy. The recent period had been mainly quiescent. Conflicts had been relatively few; most were little more than skirmishes. That couldn't last. Sooner or later, tumescent male urges would lead to something bigger. The only question was where and between whom? One likely candidate had to be the Orsonians. Their "victory" over the defenceless Mandrinians had given them a taste for conquest. Any attempt to annex Nullarbor would inevitably draw them into conflict with the Southern Cross Federation. Much worse, it would threaten the neutral zone that lay between them. Both sides would feel that they had to move into the zone before the other, and that could mean the end for the Feminarchs. They had to be stopped – but how?

"What do we think the Orsonians will do? Do they know what de la Beche was really up to yet?" asked Orestia.

"Apparently not," replied Junipa, "according to the information we have so far. That buffoon of an Admiral is still preening himself as *Lord* High Admiral, after de la Beche initiated him into what he calls the 'nobility'. You have to laugh, but I can't imagine he won't ever find out. Sooner or later the penny must drop. Then he will be after de la Beche's blood."

Orestia allowed herself a chuckle.

"Normally we wouldn't care, but we need de la Beche to find that Kwokkah. It's probably the only way the Nullarboreans might be persuaded to stay with the Southern Cross. Do we think it actually exists?"

"A very good question," said Junipa. "The Nullarboreans certainly think it exists, which in a way is the same thing, at least until they find out otherwise."

"Hmmm, so what is de la Beche doing now?"

"We have heard from one of our informants in the Southern Cross that he has gone to a planet called Libertania."

"Libertania? Never heard of it. Why has he gone there?"

"That we don't know. It's a planet way out in the back of beyond. Apparently it's the haunt of old pirates, crooks and renegades. Nobody bothers to look for them there."

Orestia could not resist another chuckle.

"It sounds just the place for his retirement, but I can't imagine he's quite ready for that yet. There must be another reason. We need to find out."

They sat in silence gazing at the incoming messages. They came in a never-ending stream – cries for help, tales of male oppression and always the suffocating blanket of religion, with all its bigotry. Eventually, Orestia spoke.

"Do you ever get depressed?"

Junipa's eyes widened in surprise.

"About what?"

"About all this. Will we ever win?"

Junipa hesitated.

"Sometimes ... it can seem overwhelming but ... I still have faith."

"In our glorious revolution?"

"In our glorious revolution – and it will be glorious."

8

Jim and de la Beche emerged from the Courthouse and walked towards the outskirts of Davy Jones. After a short distance, Jim caught sight of Mr Betelgeuse and Dr Culpepper sitting on a bench. Culpepper was mopping his brow in the hot, humid air and taking swigs from a bottle he was holding.

"Now, Jim," said de la Beche, "I know you've had a bit of a fright, but there's no time to lose. You see I've brought the old guard with me. Wisdom and experience, that's what needed here. Utrophia, here we come. That's the cry. If there's anyone here who knows how to get there, we need to find them. It won't be easy and we'll need a bit of swash, not to mention a modicum of buckle, while we're at it. I did think of bringing some of our own, but this is a tricky mission. Where would they start? We need to recruit a few locals who know the lie of the land. I think we need to visit that tavern of yours. Where better to look, in this nest of villains and cutthroats?"

Jim thought he ought to mention Schickelgrosser.

"Frankly, I've half a mind to leave him to his fate. From what you told us, he might prefer that, too."

As they entered the main street, a few of the loafers and hangers-on made low jeering noises and a few wolf-whistles. They were returned by de la Beche with a haughty wave. Jim led them to the *Dead Man's Chest*. De la Beche brushed aside the tavern swing doors, ignoring the security guards at the entrance, who could only gape at the sight, and strode up to the bar. As he did so, the entire room fell gradually silent and all eyes turned towards him. He gestured to the barman.

"Landlord, if you will, please serve drinks to all here present, with my compliments."

The barman stared at him, as if unsure of what he had heard. Eventually he responded.

"You sure you've got the money?"

De la Beche he gave him a withering stare.

"Do I look as if I am in the habit of making expansive gestures while impecunious, darling?"

The barman was still not convinced.

"What sort of money are we talking about? Southern Cross Astros? Sagittarian Bistros?"

"Now you are piling insult on ignorance. I deal only in the best – Galactos, Galactic Units of Account. In the circles in which I move, you couldn't buy a loaf of bread with a barrow-load of the pecuniary ordure that you mentioned. I take it that will be good enough for you?"

The barman assented, rather grudgingly, but the rest of the assembly were considerably more enthusiastic. They thronged the bar, eager for their free drinks, and soon the barman had to summon more staff to cope with the rush. Eventually, when more or less all had been served, de la Beche leapt on a chair, and raised his arm, calling for silence. All eyes turned towards him.

"I am Captain *Sir* Sechaverell Horatio Frobisher de la Beche, *bart*, master of HMS *Bountiful*, the most respected – *and feared* – privateer in the Galaxy. Many of you will have heard of me, a few may still be wallowing in ignorance, which I trust has now been dispelled."

Murmurs of surprise, wonder and a few cheers rose from the drinkers.

"Now, I and my colleagues are here on a very important mission, the nature of which I am not at liberty to disclose, but we are looking to recruit a few, a very few, to come with us on this mission. We are looking for those who display drive, initiative and above all superb fighting qualities, which I am sure many of you here possess."

Jim scanned the assembled faces, trying to discern which of them displayed the qualities that de la Beche had listed. He wasn't sure if he recognized any, but then thought he was not sure what to look for. De la Beche gestured towards a table in the corner of the bar.

"We will be interviewing anyone wishing to join at that table. Make your way over there and form an orderly queue."

The drinkers dispersed slowly, most appearing to give the corner table a wide berth. Eventually, Jim saw that only two figures had made their way there. De la Beche turned to the barman.

"What's the matter with these people, darling? Have they lost all their go?"

The barman gave the nearest thing he could to a guffaw.

"Go? You must be joking. They're thieves and villains. They don't want to get mixed up in anything dicey like secret missions. Too much like hard work."

De la Beche sighed.

"Whatever is the Galaxy coming to? Well, let's see what the wind has borne us."

They went over to the corner table. Jim looked the first applicant up and down and saw a slightly stooping, bow-legged figure with a weather-beaten face and white hair and beard, wearing a peaked cap, leather jerkin, baggy bell-bottoms and what looked like a bird on his shoulder. He shook hands vigorously with de la Beche.

"Well, darling, do tell us all about yourself. I can see there's a lot to tell."

The figure nodded.

"Benjamin Bones, Cap'n. I used to be bosun to Cap'n Sloakum. You might have heard of him."

De la Beche's brows furrowed.

"Sloakum the pirate?"

"The very same, Cap'n. I was bosun on his ship, the *Rum, Sodomy and the Lash*."

"Were you, indeed? I heard he was a hard taskmaster."

"That he was, Cap'n, that he was. He'd string you up soon as look at you and sometimes he'd have a poor sailor strung up when he wasn't looking, just to keep the rest of them on their toes."

De la Beche nodded appreciatively.

"And the men loved him for it, I suppose."

Bones shook his head.

"No they hated him, Cap'n, and he hated them back even worse, every man jack of them, but where could they go? No one else would have them. Besides, there was always plenty of prizes with Cap'n Sloakum. He always tossed them enough to keep them on board."

De la Beche looked at his companions.

"Would anyone else like to ask a question?"

Mr Betelgeuse indicated he had a query.

"Would you care to tell us, Mr Bones, why you left Captain Sloakum's employ?"

Bones stared at Mr Betelgeuse for several seconds, looking as if he hadn't quite understood, before he finally replied.

"I was marooned. Tell the truth, it was my own fault, really. We was on this little planet, forget its name, celebrating after we'd bagged a big 'un – a Cassiopian freighter loaded with goodies. The party lasted for days and I don't mind admitting I was well out of it most of the time. At the end I woke up and they was all gone. Ain't seen hide nor hair of them since."

Mr Betelgeuse seemed to find this interesting.

"So do you know where Captain Sloakum is now?"

Bones looked alarmed.

"There's some as say he's dead and there's some as say he ain't, but I ain't so sure. I tell ye this, Cap'n," he said, turning to de la Beche, "I'm more afear'd of Sloakum dead than any man alive – begging yer pardon, of course."

Dr Culpepper, who had seemed to be more interested in his drink during most of the interview, suddenly became animated.

"That is a particularly fine specimen of *Aratinga solstitialis,* if I'm not mistaken."

Bones' alarm grew.

"Begging yer pardon, Sir."

Culpepper smiled and raised his glass.

"The parrot on your shoulder. What's its name?"

"Doris, Sir, only it ain't no parrot, it's a psittacoid."

Culpepper sat back, puzzled.

"Whatever do you mean by psittacoid?"

Bones turned his head and made a soothing noise to the form on his shoulder.

"It's not a real bird. It's a mechanical marvel that looks like a real bird, only better."

Culpepper chuckled and took a swig from his glass.

"Well, it certainly had me fooled. How did you come by this mechanical marvel?"

Bones hesitated, looking in turn at his interviewers.

"That's a bit of a long story."

De la Beche encouraged him.

"Do tell, darling. We're all ears."

Bones sat back in his chair and drew breath.

"Well, ye see, there was this band of toymakers on the planet Ludo – long way from here, it is. They was wonderful craftsmen; could do anything mechanical – animals, birds, people, you name it. One of their toys was a stick that had a little doll in the shape of the High Admiral of Orson on the top of it – ye might have heard of him."

"We certainly have. Carry on."

"Calls hisself Lord High Admiral now, so I hear. I dunno about that, but Lord Very High Opinion of hisself he certainly is. The stick had a monkey on it. When you pressed a button, it shinned up the stick and gave the Lord High Admiral a good seeing to up the rear – if you'll pardon the expression. Best seller it was."

De la Beche allowed himself a smile.

"Most amusing. Do tell us where we can get one."

Bones shook his head, sadly.

"'Fraid you can't, Cap'n, not one of the originals anyway. They don't make 'em no more. See, when the Lord High Admiral got to hear about it, he was mad. Didn't see the funny side of things at all. So he got on to Cap'n Sloakum and asked him to make 'em see the error of their ways. We was only supposed to put it about a bit, break a few legs and arms, crack a few skulls, but what with it being one of Cap'n Sloakum's gizzard-slittin' days ..."

De la Beche gave a start.

"A what?"

Bones grimaced.

"Some days, Cap'n Sloakum would wake up and say to me, 'I feel like slittin' a few gizzards today, Bosun,' and then you had to watch out, else the gizzard he slit could be your'n. Well it was one of them days. Things got a bit out of hand and we ended up topping the lot. Right mess it was. Cap'n Sloakum made me go round totting up the bodies for the paperwork. You had to have the paperwork spot on, else the Orsonians would never pay up. They're right nit-pickers that way."

De la Beche nodded.

"We know all about the Orsonians' little ways, darling. Nit-picking and penny-pinching don't begin to describe it."

Bones continued with his tale.

"Under one of 'em, I found Doris. I said to myself, 'Benjy Bones, she's a norphan now, with no one to take care of her, only ye.' So I took her back to the ship. Cap'n Sloakum didn't take to her at first. 'What's that mangy bag o' feathers doin' round yer neck, Bosun?' he said to me. 'That's Doris, Cap'n,' I said to him, 'she's a norphan.' That set him off. 'We don't have no norphans on this ship, Bosun,' he said to me, 'nor no widders neither, case ye hadn't noticed. We *makes* widders 'n norphans on this ship. We don't collect 'em.' So I had to think of something quick. 'She's a lucky charm, Cap'n,' I said. 'She's the only one left after all the others got done.' He couldn't say nothing to that. He was very leery of Lady Luck, was Cap'n Sloakum. Didn't like to do nothing to cross her."

The *Bountiful* crew sat for several moments, contemplating Bosun Bones' tale. Then Dr Culpepper spoke.

"You say Doris is a 'mechanical marvel,' but what does she actually *do*?"

Bones nodded vigorously.

"Lots of things. For a start, she psits."

Culpepper was not enlightened.

"Psits?"

"She psits on my shoulder and psees."

Culpepper was even less enlightened.

"Psits? Psees? What are you talking about?"

"Well sir, she psits and she psees everything. She can psee through walls, round corners, anywhere you like. She tells me everything what's going on."

De la Beche's interest was piqued,

"Fascinating, darling. Would she care to tell us as well?"

Bones shook his head.

"No, she only talks to me, Cap'n."

Culpepper snorted and took another swig.

"Are there any other feats this 'marvel' can perform?"

"Yes indeed, sir. She can pswear."

Jim had to smile at that. Bones seemed almost affronted.

"Let me tell you, gents, that pswearing can come in very useful. You must have come across the Terracotti before. Biggest pests in the Galaxy. They get everywhere, thieving, doing no end of damage. We always had them hanging round when we was in dock, always after something. If Cap'n Sloakum caught one, he'd have them dangling from the bowsprit double quick. Well one day, when the Cap'n was ashore, as he liked to say, I caught a couple of 'em trying to break in to our stores. I was about to have 'em strung up when Doris started pswearing in their own lingo. Normally they'd take no notice of anything you said, but in a couple of seconds they was on their knees, weeping and wailing and promising to do anything I wanted. So I set them to swabbin' the decks. Cap'n Sloakum was always very partic'lar about having a clean ship. By the time they finished, the decks was so shiny you had to have dark glasses on to look at them. When Cap'n Sloakum came back he said to me, 'Your swabbin's lookin' up, Bosun. Keep this up and I might change my mind about havin' you keel 'auled.'"

"Very gracious of him," acknowledged de la Beche. "I think we can all agree that Doris is indeed a wonder of the age. Now, who else do we have here?"

He turned towards a tall, thin young person dressed in a long coat, pantaloons tucked inside knee-length boots and a scarf across his forehead. From his belt hung a scabbard. On being addressed, he drew a long, thin sword from the scabbard and waved it in the general direction of the company.

"They call me the Bold Deceiver. Have at you, Sirrah."

De la Beche appeared unmoved.

"Do put that thing down, darling. Didn't anyone tell you it's rude to point? Now tell us more about yourself."

The sword remained defiantly aloft.

"The Bold Deceiver, Sirrah, is the terror of the tyrannical rich, the protector of the deserving poor and the desire of every maiden. No pocket unpicked; no purse unstrung; no damsel unwooed."

De la Beche nodded appreciatively.

"Quite the busy bee, aren't we? I suspect we are all quaking in our boots. Quivering rich and swooning females are all very well, but could you tell us what you have actually *done?*"

The figure drew back, still pointing the sword.

"Done, Sirrah? *Done*! Why I unmasked the evil Drogon of Arithmethetea. I defenestrated the tyrannical Grand Vizier of Despotica. I slew the one hundred monstrous Snellnooks of the Halls of Croesovia. My fame echoes throughout the Galaxy."

"Does it indeed, darling? I must be getting a bit deaf these days, because I'm afraid I have never heard of you, or indeed of those dreadful creatures that you mentioned. Did they actually exist?"

The figure leapt back, then forward, waving his sword in agitation.

"Who dares question the Bold Deceiver? I shall have satisfaction, Sirrah! Name your weapons and appoint your seconds. I shall see you at dawn."

De la Beche smiled benignly.

"Now, darling, don't get upset. Come and sit down. We can all see you're a feisty one. Just what we're looking for. Do join us."

The Bold Deceiver stared at de la Beche for several seconds before slowly lowering his sword and putting it back into the scabbard. He sat down and took the proffered drink. Jim thought he looked younger sitting down, and rather doubted that he could slay a hundred anything, still less one hundred monstrous Snellnooks, whatever they might be. De la Beche laid a hand on his shoulder.

"Well, darling, welcome on board. And you, too, Mr Bones. If we can have a cabin boy, we can have a bosun. I'm sure there must be plenty of bosunning to be done on the *Bountiful*. Now we have to move on. We need to find out how we might get to Utrophia and I suppose we should find out what happened to the Major. Where should we start?"

Jim suggested asking the barman. He seemed to know more than he let on. De la Beche agreed and strode over to the bar.

"Now, darling, I can see you're someone who knows what's what. I'm looking for information, and I'm willing to pay, but that information has to be good. Woe betide you, if you cross me."

The barman looked at him warily.

"How much?"

"Ten Galactos. More than it's probably worth, but I'm in a generous mood."

"What do you want to know?"

"I want to go to Utrophia and I want someone to tell me how to get there."

The barman pursed his lips.

"You don't want much, do you? Some say Utrophia don't exist; then again, some say it does. Who knows?"

De la Beche eyed him disparagingly.

"Is that the best you can do? Hardly worth the price of a glass of water. I was told that someone round here knows how to get to Utrophia. Are you sure you don't know who?"

The barman shook his head.

"No idea. The only ones that might know are the Coders, and you won't get anything out of them."

"The Coders? Who are they?"

The barman shrugged.

"Who knows? Pointy heads. Think they're a cut above the rest of us. Keep themselves to themselves. They never come in here. I don't think anyone's ever seen them."

De la Beche looked at his face, judging whether he was telling the truth.

"So is anyone here acquainted with them?"

"Maybe Digobert might know." He called across the room. "Hey Dig, over here a minute."

A slightly stooped figure with long, dank hair rose from his chair and shambled over.

"Dig, you know the Coders, don't you?" said the barman.

Digobert gave a grunt.

"Depends what you mean by 'know'. We deliver to them, but I ain't never seen them."

"And what exactly do you deliver to them?" asked de la Beche.

"Pizzas, of course."

"Do enlighten me, darling. I'm afraid I come from far distant shores. What exactly is a 'pizza'?"

Digobert looked surprised.

"A pizza is a pizza. It's round and got cheese and a topping on top."

De la Beche gave a half smile.

"Sounds perfect for plugging leaks in pipes. Or do we have a clue here? Cheese? Is this pizza meant to be eaten in some way? What sort of cheese are we talking about?"

Digobert shrugged.

"I dunno. Cheese is cheese; it's sort of soft and stretchy."

"Soft and stretchy – how very exotic. Does this cheese have a provenance? Does it indeed come from an animal?"

Digobert was becoming exasperated.

"I dunno that, either. How do I know where cheese comes from? I just order it, slap it on the pizzas and send them out. What do you expect? I've got a business to run."

De la Beche decided it was best to change the subject

"How do you deliver, if you haven't seen them?"

"I just leave them outside. When I turn round, they're gone. Dunno how they do it."

De la Beche's brows furrowed.

"What do you mean 'gone'? Do they take them in through a door or a hatch or what?"

"I didn't see no door or hatch or even a window. Just walls."

De la Beche looked sceptical.

"How many of these Coders are there? How many of these pizzas do you deliver?"

"Sometimes it's two, sometimes it's twenty or anything in between. We just deliver the order. They're good payers though," he added. "Always on the nail. More than could be said for some I could name."

De la Beche thought for a few moments and then put a five Galacto token on the bar.

"I'm being over-generous as usual. Treat yourself both to libations of your choice. Now, where might I find these Coders?"

"They hang out in a joint called the Tesseract. It's just down the street." Digobert waved his arm in the general direction. "You can't miss it. It looks like a lot of boxes piled on one another at all sorts of angles. Makes my eyes go funny looking at it."

"Thank you, darling. I think we may have to pay a visit to this Tesseract." He turned to the barman. "There's one other thing you might be able to help me with. I'm told that one of my associates was in here recently and was lured somewhere by a young female, never to be seen again. Do you have any idea what might have happened to him?"

The barman gave a little snort. "Are you talking about the old geezer, claimed he was a soldier and was shooting off his mouth about how he liked killing?"

De la Beche had to agree that it sounded like the Major. The barman shook his head.

"He's gone for rat-baiting."

The puzzled look on de la Beche's face suggested to the barman that he needed to explain.

"Rat-baiting. It's a big sport round here. They've bred some very big, very vicious rats. Very nasty critters they are. There's a ring with a little kennel in it. They put someone in the kennel and then let the rats in. The rats have to drag him out. Everyone bets on it. Great fun."

"Sounds delightful. So you have young females in here luring the gullible? I assume they are paid for their efforts?"

The barman nodded.

"Circe's a great girl, but everyone's got to live.'

"So what happens to them after this rat-baiting?"

"They're not much use after three or four goes in the ring."

"And then?"

The barman shrugged and gestured with open palms.

"Take a guess."

9

However Jim viewed the building, he could not be sure of its exact shape. Parts that appeared to project seen from one angle seemed to be inset when viewed from another. An element that appeared to be above another when looked at with the right eye closed became underneath it when viewed with his other eye. It seemed to shimmer; sometimes it had a yellowish hue, sometimes blue or red, but it was never quite clear what colour it was, or if it had any colour at all. From a distance, there seemed to be no obvious opening. As they came near, a voice intoned from the wall, "Please select your preferred numeral system: two, eight, ten, twelve, twenty or sixty."

They all stopped and stared for a few seconds. Then de la Beche replied.

"I have no idea what you are talking about, darling. We have come to see those that call themselves Coders. Are you going to let us in?"

"Please select your preferred numeral system: two, eight, ten, twelve, twenty or sixty."

"I've suddenly developed an aversion to even numbers. How about thirteen?"

"Thirteen is not acceptable as the basis for a numeral system Please select from the following options: two ..."

De la Beche had had enough.

"Right, you win; twelve."

"Twelve is acceptable. You are allowed entry."

A door appeared in the wall and swung open. They hesitated for a few seconds before de la Beche led the way in, followed by Mr Betelgeuse, Dr Culpepper and Jim. Bosun Bones and the Bold

Deceiver were instructed to wait outside, but to be prepared to enter in case of emergencies. Dr Culpepper took a swig from his flask, before making up the rear. As the door closed, they saw that they had entered a large room, featureless except for the words that glowed on one wall:

"You are always a dimension away from reality."

"De la Beche turned to his First Officer.

"One for you, I think, Mr Betelgeuse. What do you make of that?"

Jim stared hard at Mr Betelgeuse, but his impassive face revealed nothing of what he was thinking.

"It does beg the question of how many dimensions those viewing those words imagine they inhabit, Captain. It might be implying that however many, there are always yet more. Indeed, some have asserted that the number of dimensions is infinite."

De la Beche waved a hand dismissively.

"I think you are over-egging the pudding, Mr Betelgeuse. Frankly, I think it's portentous nonsense."

Just then, they heard a voice behind them.

"Well, hello."

They turned and saw a figure stretched out languidly on a *chaise longue*, smoking a large hookah. As Jim looked more closely, he saw that it was some sort of apparition, probably a hologram, but it was flat: all surface, without any depth. Viewed sideways, it was invisible. It spoke again.

"You have chosen twelve as your preferred numeral system. I am the quintessence of the duodecimal."

Jim decided it was his turn to speak.

"I don't see how you could be the quintessence of anything. You are only two-dimensional; you have no substance."

The figure seemed unabashed.

"On the contrary, I have twelve dimensions, but only two are visible – and of course my dimensions are complex. I take it you have know of quaternions?"

"I'm afraid we have never been introduced, darling." said de la Beche, "Who or what are these creatures?"

"They are mathematical objects, held in the highest esteem by those of us who care about such things. I see that you do not. Three dimensions are more than enough for you. I am twelve squared, one hundred and forty-four in the decimal system that I presume in your unenlightened state you adopt. My name is Grosse Calabi-Yau."

De la Beche decided to cut things short.

"Let's not quibble about dimensions, darling. Two or twelve, it's all the same to us. We wish to speak to the Coders. How do we go about it?"

Grosse Calabi-Yau sucked several times on the hookah before replying. Jim pondered the question of inhalation in two dimensions. How exactly could it be expelled?

"First things first. Did you know that twelve is the smallest number with four non-trivial divisors and the smallest to have the first four numerals as factors?"

"Fascinating, darling. I'm sure twelve is a wonderful number; I've said so dozens of times, but where do we find the Coders?"

Grosse continued to draw slowly on the hookah.

"It is indeed most remarkable. It is a highly superior composite number, as I have just pointed out. It is the best of all number systems because its fractions are short. None of the dreadful recurring monstrosities you get with decimal. How you cope with them, I cannot begin to imagine."

De la Beche was becoming exasperated.

"We do our best. Needs must and all that. Now, *please*: the Coders. Tell us how to find them."

Jim watched as the smoke from the hookah drifted silently upwards. He tried to make out whether it was two-dimensional too, but could not be quite sure. After a few more puffs, Grosse replied.

"You do not find the Coders. The Coders may find you ... or they may not."

He turned again to his hookah and continued drawing, as his image began slowly to fade until it disappeared and all that remained was the merest wisp of smoke. Then, suddenly, the party found itself outside, on the street. They looked around, startled. Dr Culpepper took an extra large swig.

"What the devil happened?"

Mr Betelgeuse was the first to respond.

"I fear they are playing dimensional tricks on us, Doctor. A tesseract, as you may know, is a four-dimensional object with cubes as all its faces. The Coders appear to be able to manipulate dimensions. As you might see from this building, there is something curious about its appearance. I believe we have been transported through what seems a solid wall by way of a fourth spatial dimension. Most interesting."

De la Beche was less impressed.

"What I'm interested in, Mr Betelgeuse, is talking to these Coders, whoever or whatever they might be, and we don't seem to be getting anywhere." He looked around and realized someone was missing. "Where's Jim?"

Jim was not to be seen. They looked to Mr Betelgeuse.

"In my opinion, Captain, there are two possible explanations. Either the dimensional transportation sent him elsewhere ..."

"What do you mean, elsewhere?" interjected de la Beche.

"In principle, he could be anywhere in the Universe."

The party pondered this prospect.

"Or," continued Mr Betelgeuse, "he might still be in the Tesseract."

Their eyes turned towards the Tesseract, but there was no sign of an entrance or exit.

10

Jim was startled to find his companions had disappeared. He was even more startled to find the bare walls of the room suddenly replaced by what looked like stone columns and porticos, its walls covered with rich tapestries, frescoes and gold leaf. Then triumphal music sounded, and in marched a column of gaudily-dressed flunkeys, headed by a creature resplendent in a long, flowing, richly-patterned dress and cloak, wearing a crown. She looked sternly at Jim.

"Number?"

Jim swallowed hard before he was able to reply.

"What do you mean by number? Who are you?"

She looked at him even more sternly.

"Any more of that insolence and I will have your head."

Loud clucking noises came from her attendants and a bugle sounded a rasping note.

"Lord Chamberlain!"

A flunkey, even more gaudily attired than the others, dressed in hose and doublet, with a feather in his cap, stepped forward and bowed low and obsequiously.

"Your Most Excellent Numeracy."

"Summon the Executioner. I may have need of his services."

The Lord Chamberlain bowed even deeper and more obsequiously than before.

"Your Sublime Infinity's wish is my command."

He rushed off and appeared a minute later, leading a burly, shambling apparition wearing a mask and carrying a large axe.

She looked on him with some disdain.

"Executioner, is your axe sharp?"

The Executioner ran his finger along the blade.

"One, two, three, four, five, six, seven
One quick swish and they're off to..."

She interrupted him sharply.

"Enough of your ditties!"

Turning to Jim, she asked again.

"Now, give me your number."

Jim looked at the axe and swallowed even harder.

"What do you mean by number?"

Exasperated, she stamped her foot.

"You must be a simpleton. A number is a number. Everyone has a number. How old are you?"

Jim was relieved to be able to answer.

"Fifteen."

She looked at him pityingly and shook her head.

"Then you are not in your prime. What will you be next?"

Puzzled, Jim hesitated before replying.

"Why sixteen, of course."

"There is no 'of course' about it. When you are sixteen you will be even less in your prime."

Jim was more puzzled than ever.

"What do you mean by 'in my prime'?"

"You are such a simpleton. Do you know nothing? I am twenty-three. I am in my prime. Next I shall be twenty-nine, then thirty-one." She looked down at him haughtily. "I am always in my prime."

Jim thought that did not make sense.

"That doesn't make sense."

She stamped her foot, angrily this time.

"Sense! What do you know about sense? Clearly there is only nonsense that goes on in your head – and insolence. I will have you address me with my proper title."

Jim flinched.

"What is your proper title?"

"I have many – Excellent Numeracy, Sublime Infinity, Ultimate Asymptote, Magnificent Summation, too many to recite here. You must choose one."

Jim thought hard.

"I would choose Your Ultimate Asymptote."

She gave a short hrrmph.

"That is a start, but why are you such a simpleton? What have you been taught? Not much I would say, judging by the look of you."

Jim thought that was unfair, but her look had flushed Jim's mind of almost all its contents. He struggled hard to think of something to say, but very little came. Eventually he was able to blurt out, "I've been taught lots of things, like mathematics."

Her look turned to scorn.

"Who cares for mathematics? I was talking about numbers. What is one and one?"

Jim was puzzled, but he had to reply.

"Two."

She waved her arm dismissively.

"There you are. That settles it. You know nothing of numbers. One and one is very rarely two. Everyone knows that."

Jim was even more puzzled.

"What do you mean ... Your Ultimate Asymptote?"

"Do I have to explain everything?" she said, witheringly. "What is one cat and one mouse?"

"Pardon?"

"If you have one cat and one mouse, the cat will eat the mouse and then you just have one cat. Try another. What is one cat and one dog?"

Jim was about to say something, but she answered for him.

"The dog will chase the cat and they will both disappear. Want another? What is one rabbit and one other rabbit? Very soon, more rabbits that you know what to do with."

Her attendants burst into applause and singing, while buglers sounded a fanfare. Jim began to see dimly what she was getting at, but was not prepared to let things go at that.

"I'm talking about numbers, not animals. Numbers are abstract; they're not real. You can add them, subtract them, do what you like with them. So, with numbers, one and one is two ... Your Ultimate Asymptote."

That provoked even more scorn.

"Numbers not real? Whoever told you that? Of course they are real. Some of my most loyal subjects are numbers. I have just knighted Eight as a reward for gallantry. One and one is just one and one. Two is something entirely different. Two would be appalled to hear that you were accusing her of being one and one."

More applause and fanfares. Jim was beginning to think that he was running out of arguments.

"No, Your Ultimate Asymptote, I'm talking about *Arithmetic*. In Arithmetic, one and one is definitely two."

"Stuff and nonsense. Wherever did you get that notion from? When I do a sum in Arithmetic, it adds up to exactly what I say it adds up to, neither more nor less."

"The question is," said Jim, "whether you can decide to make a sum add up to anything you like."

"The question is," she replied, "whether *you* can decide that *I* can't. Besides, Arithmetic is *undecidable*. Everyone knows that."

Jim wasn't sure that he knew it.

"Who says so, Your Ultimate Asymptote?"

"The Theorems."

"What Theorems?"

"*The* Theorems. The Theorems are also among my most loyal subjects. They take it very badly when anyone doubts them. Your life would hardly be worth living, if you did."

Jim tried hard to recall the little logic he had once been taught.

"I think, Your Ultimate Asymptote, you mean that some statements in Arithmetic may be undecidable."

She shrugged off Jim's interpretation.

"Some or all, who gives a fig? One and one is definitely among them."

"Pardon me, Your Ultimate Asymptote, but who decided that?"

"I did."

"So, you decide what is undecidable?"

She glared at him.

"Of course I do. Who else would decide? Not you, surely? I frequently decide six undecidable things before breakfast."

Jeers and catcalls for Jim came from the attendants; the bugles sounded again. He tried one last query.

"Isn't that a contradiction, Your Ultimate Asymptote? If something is undecidable, you can't decide it. If you can decide it, then it's not undecidable."

"Not at all. You clearly do not know your numbers. Some numbers, I grant you, are quite decided. Even numbers nearly always know what they are, but odd numbers are an entirely different kettle of fish. They have absolutely no idea of anything. That's why they are called odd. You must know that."

Jim had to confess that he didn't. She looked at him scornfully.

"Executioner, off with his head. He won't miss it. There's nothing inside."

The noise from the attendants rose to a crescendo; the bugles sounded a triumphant fanfare. The Executioner readied his axe and the Lord Chamberlain danced a jig, whirling round and round, cap in hand. Jim stood frozen in fear but then, through the tears that he could not prevent from welling up, he saw the whole scene slowly disappear and the noise fade to silence.

11

Jim sat for a while in the featureless room, trembling, almost unable to move. Little by little he began to feel better and realized that he was feeling very hungry. He could not remember the last time he had eaten.

Just then, the scene changed again. He found himself looking at a large, elaborately-wrought iron gate set in a high stone wall. On the gate was a notice:

The Paradox Cafe
Always open
All welcome

Through the gate, he saw what appeared to be a long table on a veranda, overhung with trees and creepers, on which was a huge assortment of food of all sorts – pies, cakes, meats, puddings, fruit and much else, together with an equally large variety of drinks. Sitting at the table he could see three figures.

The figures did not look threatening, but given his experience so far, he was not keen to take chances. On the other hand, he was *very* hungry. A rope hung down at the side of the gate and a small notice said "Pull for attention." He pulled and a bell sounded. One of the figures rose and approached the gate. The figure was large, corpulent and its gait a little unsteady. He saw Jim and waved him at him.

"Yes?"

"I would like to come in, please."

"The cafe is closed. Go away."

Jim was taken aback. This was not what he expected, given the notice on the gate.

"But it says here that you are always open."

"Well," said the figure, "even if we were open, we wouldn't let you in."

"But it says 'All welcome'."

The figure shook his head.

"What is this cafe called?"

"The Paradox Cafe, so it says."

"That's your answer," said the figure and started back towards the table.

Jim stared at the retreating figure and then at the table. The sight of the food made his hunger all the more acute. He decided to try again and pulled on the bell. The figure returned.

"What do you want now?"

"What if I said I didn't want to come in?"

The figure nodded.

"Well, do you want to come in?"

"No, and I wouldn't come in even if you asked me."

The gate was swung open.

"Welcome."

The two of them walked back to the table. The first figure sat down and began the introductions.

"I'm Red and these two are Ad and Abs. We're members of the philosophical fraternity. I am the paragon of paradox, Ad is the connoisseur of contradictions and Abs is the nabob of nonlinearity."

"Very pleased to meet you." said Jim. He eyed a particularly delicious-looking slice of meat pie. His expression clearly indicated desire. Abs held him back.

"You must order from the waiter. You can have anything you like."

Jim was surprised. He could see food enough on the table for an army, let alone for three. He looked around and, just behind him, seemingly appearing from nowhere, was a figure in a black jacket and long white apron who he assumed was the waiter. The waiter leant forward slightly, his manner formal.

"Oui, monsieur?"

Jim was not sure what he meant, but went ahead and ordered anyway. He selected goodly portions of meats, pudding and fruit, to be washed down with his favourite cordial. When he had finished ordering he realized that there was no chair for him to sit on and no room on the table to put his food. He pointed this out to the waiter.

"Pas de problème, monsieur. This is the *Table d'Hilbert.* It is an infinite table. We just move everyone and everything up a little and there will be plenty of room for you and your order."

He nodded gravely and went off. Jim looked down the table and realized that he could not see its end. The table, trees and creepers disappeared into the distance. From the distant noise of conversation and tinkling of glasses, he became aware that there were other diners, although he could not quite make them out. Red, Ad and Abs shifted in their chairs and a seat became vacant for him.

As he waited for his food, Jim studied his companions more closely. Red, he saw, was corpulent, slightly sweaty and wore a singlet with a drawing of an ever-ascending staircase. Ad was thinner and on his singlet was written "Who is the square root of minus infinity?" Abs was very tall and skinny. He wore a top hat, a black jacket with tails, a ruched shirt and a large silk cravat. The food arrived and Jim ate ravenously, as they looked on in silence. After a few minutes, he felt a little better and thought he should start the conversation.

"Can I ask a question?"

"Fire away," said Abs.

"You will promise to tell me the truth?"

"Of course, " said Red. "We're all liars here."

Jim was taken aback.

"That doesn't make sense. If you say you are liars then either you are telling the truth that you are liars or you are lying – in which case you are telling the truth."

Red beamed.

"Got it in one, young sir. I am paradox personified. I deal in nothing else."

"But you've just said you are a liar, so you must deal in other things."

"Precisely. That's the beauty of paradoxes."

Frustration was beginning to get to Jim.

"That's silly. It's no way to go on. What do you three do? There can't be enough paradoxes to keep you occupied all day."

"Do?" said Abs. "We do nothing, of course. What else is there to do?"

Jim thought he spied a chink in their logic.

"You say you do nothing, but you also say you are liars, so you must do something."

"Not at all," said Ad. "Let me explain. What is the numerical equivalent of nothing?"

Jim was not sure what his point was, but decided to answer anyway.

"Zero, I suppose."

"Precisely, and what is the negative of zero?"

Jim was even less sure of the point.

"What do you mean 'negative'? Zero doesn't have a negative."

Ad smiled.

"On the contrary, the negative of zero is zero. Zero is the only number that is its own negative. So there you are: it's proven mathematically. Whether we are lying or telling the truth, when we say we do nothing, we still do nothing."

Jim was far from convinced by this line of argument, but on the other hand he could not quite see what was wrong with it. He tried another tack.

"Doing nothing must be very boring."

Red demurred.

"Not at all. If you *do* something, then that's it. It's done. But doing nothing lasts all day long. Keeps you busy. Then there are the surprises."

"Surprises?"

"Yes, every day must bring its surprises. I would have thought you knew that," said Abs.

Jim pondered this for a little while.

"So, was I a surprise?"

Red shook his head.

"No. We expect surprises, so when you turned up we weren't surprised."

Jim was baffled.

"So, how can anything be a surprise?"

"Only when it's not. I would have thought that was obvious," said Ad, in a patronizing tone of voice.

The conversation seemed to be going round in circles. Jim thought he needed something to break the circularity and then something from the previous episode occurred to him.

"Is there anything we can agree on? Let me ask you a simple question. What is one and one?"

"Ah, the peak of paradox," exclaimed Red.

"The acme of contradiction," asserted Ad.

"The apogee of nonlinearity," agreed Abs.

Jim could hardly contain his frustration.

"What do you mean? It's a very simple question. One and one is two. You must agree that it's true?"

"Of course it's true, which is why we don't believe it," said Red.

Frustration was now compounded with bafflement.

"How can you not believe something you know is true?"

"What's the point of believing something simply because it's true?" said Abs. "Any fool can do that. We consider ourselves a cut above the common herd. We prefer to believe in things that aren't true."

Jim thought things were becoming absurd and he might as well join in. He remembered the vainglorious boasts of the Bold Deceiver.

"So I suppose you know the one hundred monstrous Snellnooks of the Halls of Croesovia?"

"Of course," said Red. "Delightful fellows, every one. Won't have a word said against them."

Jim could not hold himself back.

"But they don't exist."

"All the better for it," said Red. "Existence is overrated, if you ask me. All the most unpleasant creatures of my acquaintance have existed. The ones that don't are much nicer."

Jim decided he had to give this some thought.

"Do you think I exist?"

"Of course not," replied Ad. "You're such a pleasant young man, you couldn't possibly exist, which is why we're talking to you."

"Well, *I* think I exist," said Jim in a determined tone.

"No you don't," said Red. "How could you, when you say you can think? Thinking and existing are opposite things. Can you see thinking? Or kick it or eat it or do anything at all with it? It doesn't exist. If you can think, you don't exist. Stands to reason."

Jim was pretty sure it didn't stand to reason, but again he wasn't quite sure of the exact reason to which it would fail to stand. However, he was feeling refreshed and was beginning to recover a little self-confidence, but he realized that he was not likely to get the better of the three in argument, and it would be best to change the subject. He remembered why he and the others from the *Bountiful* had entered the Tessaract in the first place, and thought he might make some enquiries.

"I came here hoping to meet the Coders. Do you know where I might find them?"

The three looked at each other and sighed.

"Dimensions, dimensions, dimensions," said Red. "It's always dimensions with the Coders. Do you have any dimensions on you?"

"Pardon?"

"Do you have any spare dimensions about your person? Space? Time? It's all the same to them."

"I don't think I do," said Jim, unsure of what a spare dimension would look like.

"Well," said Red, "then I don't think you'll have much luck with them. They do like their dimensions. Let me take a look at you and see how many you have. Turn round."

Jim stood up and turned round.

"As I thought, three of space at best," said Red. "Not enough, in my opinion."

Jim was undeterred. "I would still like to try."

"Very well, then," said Red. "You will need to leave the cafe and ask for directions."

Jim pointed to the gate where he had come in. "That way?"

"No," said Red, "that's the entrance. You can't get out that way. You need to go out of the exit." He pointed down the veranda. "It's that way."

Jim peered into the distance, but could see no sign of an exit. "How far is it?"

Red looked at him in surprise. "It's infinitely far, of course."

Jim was utterly dismayed. "I'll never reach it."

"Yes, but look on the bright side," said Abs. "You might as well stay here and enjoy yourself, because however far you went you wouldn't be any nearer the exit than you are now." He raised his glass. "Cheers!"

A sense of frustration began to overwhelm Jim. He could see no way out of his predicament. He banged his fists angrily on the table and, as he did so, the cafe began to disappear. Soon he was back in the featureless, gloomy, grey room.

12

Jim stared for ages at the walls. He could see no windows or doors, nothing that would indicate any means of escape. Then, in one corner, slowly, out of the gloom, the figure of Grosse Calabi-Yau, reclining on a *chaise longue* and smoking a hookah, began to emerge.

"Greetings," said Grosse. "I do hope you have enjoyed your recent sojourns."

Jim had to confess that he hadn't enjoyed them very much, although he admitted that the food at the Paradox Cafe was very good.

"Yes," agreed Grosse, "the Cafe and the *Table d'Hilbert* are renowned. The chefs come from a part of infinite-dimensional space where they take their food very seriously."

Jim said he was glad to hear it. Grosse looked him up and down.

"Speaking of dimensions, there are not many to you, are there?"

"What do you mean?" said Jim, a little indignantly.

"Well, what would I give you?" said Grosse, "Two and a half, maybe two and three-quarters, if I'm being generous."

"That's just silly," said Jim. "How can you have bits of dimensions? It's either two like you or three like me."

"I have twelve dimensions," said Grosse. "Two you can see, and the other ten all curled up, safe and warm. It's you who are being silly. What about a ball of string?"

Jim had no idea of what he was talking about.

"What about a ball of string?"

"How many dimensions does a length of string have?" asked Grosse.

"One, its length, I suppose."

"Roll it up into a ball. How many dimensions now?"

"Three."

"No," said Grosse emphatically. "Two and a bit. Anyone will tell you that. You're just like a ball of string. There's nothing to you. I couldn't give you three dimensions even if I wanted to. I really couldn't."

Jim thought for a few moments and then decided he would consider himself in full possession of all three of his dimensions, whatever Grosse said. However, the much more pressing question was how was he to get out of the Tesseract? He ran through in his mind a few ways to broach the question to Grosse and decided it was probably best to be explicit.

"Could you tell me how I might get out of here?"

Grosse looked very surprised.

"Why would you want to go? You have everything here."

Jim bristled.

"Everything? You mean being threatened with having my head cut off and having to walk an infinite distance?"

"Well, yes. We offer an infinity of possibilities here, so you have to take the rough with the smooth. You must see that. In fact," he added, "we offer two sorts of infinities of possibilities. The common or garden one, which is just all the numbers, and the Continuum one, which is everything in between."

Jim thought that was absurd.

"How can there be two sorts of infinity?"

Grosse took a pull on his hookah.

"If you don't know, I'm not going to tell you." He cast a somewhat critical eye over Jim. "The Continuum is much more expensive. You don't look as if you could afford it."

"I don't think I'd like either." said Jim, sarcastically. "Have you anything in between?"

Grosse gave him a supercilious look.

"That is a question above your ability to understand."

Direct questions didn't seem to be working. Jim decided to try another approach.

"Maybe you could help me. We came to see you because we thought you might be able to tell us about Utrophia."

Grosse stayed silent and sucked several times on the hookah before replying.

"Utrophia. Why would you want to know about it?"

Jim knew he had to be cautious.

"We are looking for something and we think it might be there. Do you know how we might get there?"

Grosse continued to suck on the hookah.

"I will give you a clue: Roy Pesshe."

"What do you mean, Roy Pesshe?" asked Jim, puzzled.

"I said it's a clue. It's for you to find out."

"How can I find out if I'm in here?"

Grosse gave what Jim thought might be a smile and then slowly began to fade from view. As he disappeared Jim saw written again on the wall:

"You are always a dimension away from reality."

Suddenly, the room disappeared and he found himself on the street outside the Tessaract, next to the crew of the *Bountiful*. A startled Doctor Culpepper saw him first.

"Oh there you are, Jim. For a minute, we thought we had lost you. What happened?"

13

A nagging suspicion was growing in the mind of the Lord High Admiral of the Orsonian Battle Fleet. He had tried to banish it by thinking of the particularly voluptuous *Maitresse en titre,* who he had just appointed and who had been most energetic in expressing her gratitude, but it kept coming back. The suspicion was that Captain *Sir* Sechaverell Horatio Frobisher de la Beche, *bart,* the bestower of titles upon him and his consorts, was not all he seemed.

The Admiral had been receiving unaccustomed – and, in his view, utterly unjustified – criticism from Orsonian society. After the incident with the Astromicans, there had been some entirely justified executions of the incompetent and corrupt inspectors at the Desideratan end of the operation, who had let it happen. The Desideratans, however, had taken exception to these actions and had banned all further deliveries of Chelodoney to Orson.

Naturally, since unreasoning vindictiveness is a central part of the Orsonian character, all sections of society blamed him for the absence of Chelodoney. The Orsonian chattering classes – as if they didn't have enough to chatter about – were forever complaining about the lack of their favourite food. Publishers moaned that sales of cookbooks had plummeted. Restaurateurs whined that, without Chelodoney, their customers were staying away and they would be ruined. Even his wives were saying that, without Chelodoney, the lavish banquets they gave for the high and mighty of Orson lacked sparkle.

Another central element of the Orsonian character was the propensity to blame others. Someone else must always be responsible. It was simply a matter of deciding who. The more he thought about de la Beche and his activities, the more suspicious he became. He had turned up out of the blue just when a war scare had made commercial transport of Chelodoney impossible. He had transported the Astromicans. There was that business with so-called repairs. Then he had allowed himself to be inveigled by de la Beche into agreeing to let de la Beche take the two prisoners away. He now convinced himself that he had been suspicious from the start but, in his good-natured way, had given de la Beche the benefit of the doubt. Then de la Beche had disappeared, without giving notice. Perhaps he should put out an alert across the Orsonian Empire to arrest de la Beche – or, failing that, to eliminate him.

On the other hand, he thought to himself, what if I'm wrong? De la Beche might take exception and take back his title. What would he tell his wives and mistresses? They would be furious and might decide they could do better elsewhere. He knew that a few in Orsonian high society had already made overtures to some of his more desirable females. What to do? The first principle of any well-ordered autocracy is that all messengers should be shot on sight and all stable doors locked and securely bolted, but only after ensuring no animals of any sort remain inside. The second is that subordinates are always to be blamed when things go awry. The Lord High Admiral was scrupulous in his adherence to these principles. The first thing was to find a suitably dispensable messenger.

"Civil Servant 21346, come in here at once," he barked.

Civil Servant 21346 awoke with a start from a reverie, a particularly arousing reverie, as it happened. He had bought a potion from a denizen of the Orsonian *demi-monde* who had assured him that it was guaranteed to reduce any female to a state of lustful complaisance. He imagined himself slipping it secretly to one of the Lord High Admiral's mistresses and ravishing her in one of his lordship's many gilded bedrooms. Just as his reverie was reaching its climax, the Lord High Admiral's voice induced instant detumescence. He breathed deeply several times, as his hormonal levels reduced to something like normal, then gathered himself and set off down the corridor for the Lord High Admiral's state room.

"What do you know about Captain de la Beche?" said the Lord High Admiral, in what he imagined to be an inquisitorial tone.

Civil Servant 21346 was a little surprised, since the Admiral had actually conversed with de la Beche, whereas he had not. Nevertheless, he proceeded on the maxim that no experience had ever improved, or indeed affected, the Lord High Admiral's judgement.

"I know he charges about five times what we normally pay for freight."

For once the Admiral decided to ignore Civil Servant 21346's semi-dumb insolence.

"Yes, yes, but what I want to know is, what do you *know* about him?"

"*Know* about him?"

The insolence was becoming harder to ignore, but the Admiral made a huge effort.

"Please do not keep repeating what I say, Civil Servant 21346. I want to know if there is other information that you have not told me about."

Civil Servant 21346 had to think hard, not because there was no other information, but how to phrase it most judiciously."

"Well, there were rumours."

"What rumours?"

"That he has been in contact with the Southern Cross Federation."

A surge of anger rose within the Lord High Admiral's breast. Such a surge was always induced by any mention of the Southern Cross Federation. A secondary surge then began, when he contemplated de la Beche's contact with the loathed enemy. A third came when he thought about Civil Servant 21346's concealment of the fact. Three surges was the limit to which the Admiral's anger levels could be raised before he became a quivering ball of rage.

"Why didn't you tell me about this?" he yelled, when his anger had subsided sufficiently for him to get the words out.

"Because it was mentioned in something you said I wasn't to mention."

The Lord High Admiral felt a potentially terminal fourth surge rising, but he managed to control it.

"What on Orson are you talking about?"

Civil Servant 21346 could not suppress a little gloat.

"It was in the *Galactic Inquirer.*"

The *Galactic Inquirer* was a scandal-sheet that circulated Galaxy-wide and was read avidly. It had leakers and informants everywhere. Very few secrets were safe from its prying eyes. It took particular delight in exposing the hypocrisies and peccadilloes of the powerful. It had mentioned the Lord High Admiral in less than flattering terms on many occasions. It lampooned his sense of self-importance and jeered that he was always being cuckolded by his wives and mistresses. It had even sponsored a project to resurrect the toy that featured a stick, a monkey and an effigy of the Admiral, which had become a best-seller again. As a result, the Lord High Admiral had decreed that no mention of the *Galactic Inquirer* was ever to be made in his hearing and no copies were to be allowed anywhere in the Orsonian Empire.

The ban was less than successful. Civil Servant 21346 was part of an underground communications network on which all sorts of information circulated that those in power in the Galaxy would have preferred to be kept secret. It also included titillating material catering for every conceivable taste, much of it supplied by the *Galactic Inquirer,* which was why Civil Servant 21346 was such a devotee of the network. The fact that the *Inquirer* had been mentioned meant that it was now a question of whether the

Admiral would be consumed with rage before he could find out what it had said. The Admiral gritted his teeth and, in his fury, neglected to ask how Civil Servant 21346 had come to know what was in a forbidden publication.

"What did it say?"

Civil Servant 21346 saw no point in holding anything back.

"It said that the Southern Cross Federation found out that you had something called the Kwokkah, which apparently is sacred on one of their planets, Nullarbor, and that you were using the Kwokkah to get them to come over to our empire and the Southern Cross were desperate to prevent it, so they hired de la Beche."

A mounting sense of trepidation was adding to the Admiral's anger.

"Anything else?"

Civil Servant 21346 was in gloat heaven.

"Yes. The plan was to create a war scare which meant no commercial transports would come to Orson and de la Beche would step in and agree to transport Chelodoney from Desiderata to somewhere else that we can't mention, which was where the Kwokkah was supposed to be. They had broken the seals' codes on the Chelodoney containers and hired Astromican soldiers, who would hide in the containers and take over the place that we can't mention and capture the Kwokkah. De la Beche would be waiting to take them and the Kwokkah back. Only something went wrong, and now we can't get any Chelodoney. It all sounds very unlikely to me. We wouldn't have let that happen, would we?"

It was all too much for the Lord High Admiral, who felt he could no longer restrain the bellow that had been all too long in coming. It rose like magma in a huge volcanic outburst.

"Get me Sloakum!"

14

Jim stood blinking in the unaccustomed daylight. He was surprised to find that, according to the others, he had only been missing for about a minute. He started to explain what had happened to him in the Tesseract, but only succeeded in confusing himself, as well as the others, so he gave up after mentioning the clue to the Coders that Grosse had given him. De la Beche looked as if he didn't think much of it.

"Roy Pesshe. Who or what or where is that, darling? Was your friend Grosse so good as to give you even a scintilla of enlightenment?"

Jim said he had no idea. All Grosse had said was that it was a clue. They had to work it out. De la Beche grunted.

"Mr Betelgeuse, have you ever heard any mention of a Roy Pesshe?"

Mr Betelgeuse paused for several seconds.

"Not to my knowledge, Captain. Are we dealing with a personage of some sort?"

De la Beche asked the others if they had any ideas. None ventured anything.

"We'll learn nothing just standing here. When we return to the *Bountiful* we may be able to find out more. Meanwhile, let's ask around and see if any of the unlovely denizens of this most unlovely place have anything to tell us."

Jim looked around and thought he recognized a slim, dark-haired figure walking a little distance down the road.

"That's her. The one who went off with the Major."

"Are you sure?" asked de la Beche. Jim said he was. "Well, let's start our enquiries with her. She has some explaining to do."

Just then the Bold Deceiver stepped forward.

"At your service, Sirrah. No maid unwooed by the Bold Deceiver. She will tell all in a trice."

Before anyone said anything, he bounded off. They watched as he approached the young female, removed his hat, bowed low and then appeared to say something to her. She stood looking at him for a few seconds, then drew back her arm and hit him hard in the face. He fell back on the floor.

"Interesting wooing technique the Bold Deceiver has, don't you think, Doctor?" said de la Beche. "Perhaps we should rescue him before she becomes even more amorous."

The Bold Deceiver had staggered to his feet by the time they arrived. The female did not notice their arrival until she turned round.

"Who are you?" she said in an aggressive tone and then she saw Jim. "Oh."

"*Oh* indeed, darling," said de la Beche. "I think you have some explaining to do. I understand from young Jim here that you lured one of my colleagues to a rather unsavoury fate."

"I don't know what you're talking about."

"Oh I think you do, darling. You enticed our Major Schickelgrosser, a military man, as I think he told you, into going with you and handed him over to some ruffians, who are now, so I am informed, setting a pack of vicious rodents on him."

She looked around desperately, but could see there was no escape.

"Oh, him. He was talking about how he liked killing and stuff, so I introduced him to some people I know. I thought he might like a bit of action."

"Like being torn to pieces by bloodthirsty rats?"

Her tone turned defensive.

"It's a fair fight. Well, fairish."

De la Beche smiled.

"Part of me thinks we should leave the Major to his fate. He can be a little tiresome at times. On the other hand, rats. Such an undignified end to what I'm sure was a distinguished military career. I think perhaps we should intervene on aesthetic grounds alone. Why don't we go and take a look at what has happened to him?"

She looked very surprised.

"You want to go to the rat-baiting?"

"Of course, darling. Why don't you take us there?"

They walked through the back streets of the town. They went past fast-food joints, offering comestibles from almost every planet in the Galaxy to those homesick for their very own tucker, and past saloons, gambling joints and cheap clothes stores. Eventually, they came to a small stadium; the roar of a loud, boisterous and probably inebriated crowd inside the stadium was almost deafening. A gate was open and they went through, climbed up stairs into the stadium and found seats on a bench. Jim looked down at the arena and saw, in the middle of a sawdust ring, a small hutch with an open entrance. About half a dozen rats, the size of large dogs, were running around making noises halfway between a squeak and a howl. Suddenly, one made a dash for the hutch entrance and disappeared inside. There was a series of very loud squeaks that turned to screams and the rat emerged, running with a pronounced limp, minus one ear and half its tail. The crowd roared.

Two more rats tried their luck, with much the same result. The crowd roared louder. Then a bell rang, and figures in padded suits with shields and whips entered, driving the rats into a corral at the side of the arena. A truck with a crane drove into the arena, picked up the hutch and drove out again, to cheers from the crowd. Many in the crowd went over to another area, where billboards advertised odds on the outcomes of the events, to collect their winnings.

Jim had watched the events with a horrified fascination. Bosun Bones, on the other hand, was enthusiastic.

"Best fun I've had in ages, Cap'n. Takes me back. Cap'n Sloakum used to do this sort of thing. He'd have someone swinging from the yardarm and a couple of mad dogs taking bites out of 'em. Biggest biter won. We took bets on it. I collected a fair old packet on some days, I don't mind telling you."

De la Beche turned to the female.

"What did you say your name was?"

She answered defensively.

"Circe."

"Well, Circe, darling, perhaps you could introduce us to the same people to whom you introduced the Major. I would like to have a word with them."

She looked very surprised.

"You want to meet the Ratmeister?"

"If that's who it is, yes."

She pointed to a small office by the side of the stadium.

"He's probably in there."

De la Beche nodded.

"I think you should come with us. You can make the introductions."

A look of alarm spread over Circe's face, but she realized that she had no choice. They went over to the office and de la Beche led them through the door. Sitting behind a large desk Jim saw a corpulent, red-faced man dressed in fur, which looked suspiciously like rat fur, wearing a large fur hat with a long tail running down his back. Behind him on the wall hung three trophy rat heads in aggressive poses. He looked up as he saw them enter.

"Yus?"

Then he spied Circe and his voice rose.

"If you're bringing another one, you can forget it. That last one's given me no end of grief. The rats can't get him out and the crowd won't let me get rid of him. I've lost a packet and the bookies are going to go on strike. I won't have a business much longer at this rate."

Jim saw that Circe was shaking as she answered. She pointed to de la Beche.

"He says he wants to talk to you."

The Ratmeister eyed de la Beche with a mixture of suspicion and astonishment. He seemed particularly taken aback by the crimson turban and the gold and diamond pendant.

"What do you mean, coming in here dressed like that?"

De la Beche smiled sweetly.

"Tut, tut. Manners, darling. You're hardly the belle of the ball yourself. As it happens, I'm dressed for the country. I would of course wear something a little sleeker and more chic for an evening in town, but you'll just have to take me as I am. Now, I understand you know a colleague of ours. I suspect he might be the one you were complaining of, the one who seems to be giving your rats such a hard time."

"That depends on why you're asking."

De la Beche nodded.

"Exactly so. I believe we can come to a mutually satisfactory agreement. I think we can take this troublesome individual off your hands, for a small consideration, and you can get back to running a profitable business."

The Ratmeister shook his head.

"Can't do it. The spectators would kill me. They like to see the rats given a hiding." He let out a snort of disgust. "Do you know how much it costs to train a rat? It takes ages. You've got to starve 'em and beat 'em to make 'em vicious. Then you've got to teach 'em to go into the hutch and drag whatever's in there out. It costs a fortune – and I've lost three rats this week already. Do those bastards watching care? No. They only want to see more rats cut up. At this rate I won't have none left. I'll be out of business, whatever I do."

De la Beche made sympathetic sounds.

"Our hearts bleed for you, darling. Perhaps we might be able to help. Let me tell you with whom you are dealing. I am Captain Sir Sechaverell Horatio Frobisher de la Beche, master of HMS *Bountiful*, the most feared privateer in the Galaxy; this is Mr Betelgeuse, one of the Galaxy's finest minds; this is Bosun Bones and Doris, late of the crew of Captain Sloakum, the feared pirate; this is the Bold Deceiver, the despatcher of the one hundred monstrous Snellnooks of the Halls of Croesovia, no less; and this is Jim, the cabin boy. Now I think anyone would agree that we are a fearsome band, one that even someone as steadfast and unyielding as yourself would find impossible to resist."

The Ratmeister's suspicions were rising again.

"What are you getting at? Are you saying you're going to cut my throat? I've got people here. They'll come running when I yell."

"Calm down, darling. I am giving you the perfect excuse for your spectators. All you have to do is say that we came for this individual – Major Schickelgrosser is his name – because he has committed numerous offences against us and we wished to settle scores. You tried as hard as you could to resist, but in vain. We insisted on taking him away to give him his just deserts. I'm sure the spectators will understand, and to sweeten things I will be prepared to forget about any charges on our part and donate a hundred Galactos for the welfare of those rats he has so grievously injured. What do you say?"

The Ratmeister looked warily at each of them before turning back to de la Beche.

"Make it two hundred. Patching up rats ain't cheap, I'll have you know."

De la Beche shook his head.

"You really are pushing your luck, darling. You said yourself that you would be out of business if you can't get rid of him. I tell you what, I will throw in an extra twenty as a gesture of goodwill. Positively my final offer. Take it or leave it."

The Ratmeister pursed his lips and thought for a moment.

"OK, OK, it's a deal. Only you have to get him out of here without anyone seeing."

De la Beche agreed. "Take us to him."

The Ratmeister led them to an area at the back of the office, past the rat pens, where the rats snarled and spat at them, to a small building with a large padlock on its door. He turned the key in the padlock and opened the door. Inside was an iron cage. In one corner the Major, his legs manacled, was lying on the floor. Jim saw that he had large scratches on his arms, legs and face.

"I've brought some people to see you, matey," said the Ratmeister.

Schickelgrosser did not look up and made a number of guttural sounds that Jim suspected might have been expletives.

"Don't take it like that, matey," said the Ratmeister. "This could be your lucky day. They want to take you away." He turned to de la Beche. "We keep him doped up when he's not in the ring. He don't know what he's doing or saying."

Schickelgrosser slumped back, eyes closed, still muttering to himself. De la Beche asked the Ratmeister how he suggested they could get him out of the compound without anyone seeing.

"I've been thinking about that. You could use the rat cart. It's what we take the dead rats to the dump in," he added. "It's a bit tight, but he should fit."

"So we walk out with the cart?"

The Ratmeister shook his head vigorously.

"No, not all of you. That would look like a bleedin' funeral for a rat, wouldn't it? Let him take it." He pointed at Jim. "I usually get a young lad to do it."

De la Beche assented and the Ratmeister whistled and gestured to an attendant to fetch the cart. He opened the cage, unlocked the manacles and each of them grabbed one of Schickelgrosser's limbs and hoisted him in. The Ratmeister pulled a tarpaulin over him and fastened it to the cart sides. He gestured to Jim.

"Now you just pull it nice and easy, like you hadn't a care. Go that way, like you were going to the dump, and don't let him out until you're well out of town. If he makes a noise or cuts up rough hit him with this." He produced a large cosh. "Understand?"

Jim said he understood, though he doubted that hitting the Major with a cosh would have any effect. He took the handle of the cart, which turned out to be surprisingly easy to pull, and trundled with it out of the compound and down the street. The others followed at a discreet distance.

They were some way out of town, in an area of rough scrub, when Jim stopped and the others caught up. De la Beche asked Jim to remove the cover. Schickelgrosser moaned, and his eyes screwed up in the unaccustomed light. He was stuffed so tightly into the cart that he could not move. They lifted him out and sat him on the ground. Dr Culpepper examined him and indicated that there was nothing seriously wrong. Gradually Schickelgrosser began to regain consciousness. He looked up and saw them staring at him.

"What happened? Where am I?" He shook his head as if to clear it. "I had this dream. I was being eaten alive by giant rats. I kept cutting them and they kept coming, but I kicked their damn asses in the end. But why would I have a dream like that? Giant rats, where did they come from? Never had nothing like it before."

"You do look as if you have been through the wars, darling," said de la Beche. "Perhaps Dr Culpepper could shed a little light on your predicament."

Culpepper looked surprised, took a swig from his flask and then offered it to Schickelgrosser.

"I think you have suffered from what we doctors called a psychotrauma, Major. It happens quite a lot to military men. Nothing to be ashamed of. All that combat stress can build up and then something snaps. You need to take it easy for a little while."

Schickelgrosser gave him a puzzled look.

"Well, maybe you're right, Doc. Maybe I've been hitting it a little hard lately. Last thing I remember I was in a bar, talking to this sweet little thing ..." He looked up and saw Circe. "That's her. She's the one I was talking to. Maybe she knows what happened."

"Well er, yes, you were talking to me. Showing me how you kill," said Circe, very flustered, "but then you, er, disappeared and I never saw you again."

He looked at her sadly.

"So where'd I disappear to? And how did I get like this?" he said, pointing at his wounds.

Dr Culpepper realized he needed to intervene.

"It's not uncommon with psychotrauma. You can walk into things, get into scrapes, fall over – and not remember a thing. Here, have another swig, Major. Bound to help."

Schickelgrosser took a large swig. "Yeah, maybe you're right, Doctor. Maybe that's what happened. Maybe I'll remember in a while."

De la Beche surveyed the desolate landscape, idly brushing the biting insects away.

"This place is clearly not as welcoming as it looks. I think perhaps it might be best to return to the *Bountiful* and collect our thoughts."

15

The Lord High Admiral of the Orsonian Fleet stared at the apparition before him on his screen with a mixture of distaste and disbelief, unsure which element produced the greatest aversion. Was it the bulbous nose, with its two huge, hairy warts? Or was it the one protruding, bloodshot eye – the other was covered with a black patch – from which some pus-like fluid appeared to be seeping? Then again, it might have been the long, straggly beard, encrusted with who knew what, and seemingly inhabited by crawling vermin, or the jagged rows of blackened stumps of teeth. He summoned every ounce of self- control to utter a greeting.

"Captain Sloakum. Such a pleasure to make your acquaintance again. How have things been with you?"

The apparition growled and its face took on an even more dismissive scowl.

"Bilgewater! Don't give me that 'pleasure to make your acquaintance'. We both know ye're after somethin' that the bunch of lily-livered swab rags ye call sailors are too frit to do. Call yerself an Admiral! I'd have the lot of 'em strung up before ye could powder yer fat backside."

The Lord High Admiral struggled mightily to repress a bellow. Abuse was not something he would normally tolerate, but he was aware from previous experience that Sloakum knew no other mode of discourse.

"As you surmise, Captain, I have a little task in mind that I think would be ideally suited to your particular talents."

"But not suited to my purse, I'll wager. Ye can take yer little task and stick it where no star will ever shine."

The Lord High Admiral's jaw and fists clenched in a final effort, as the urge to bellow threatened to become uncontrollable.

"Now, Captain Sloakum, a little civility would not come amiss. This particular task will I think appeal to you and I can assure you that you will be paid handsomely, if you accomplish it."

Sloakum's jaw moved from side to side and his cheeks bulged slightly, as though he was chewing something as he pondered. Eventually he spoke.

"Well, let's hear it."

The Lord High Admiral smiled inwardly. Revenge was the dish he most favoured, whether served cold, lukewarm or piping hot. Indeed, he considered that the whole point of being a Lord High Admiral was that it gave him the right to exact revenge on all who had the temerity to cross him.

"I expect you have heard of a certain Captain de la Beche?"

Sloakum sniffed.

"Talks lah-di-dah and prances round in skirts."

The Lord High Admiral considered this a sufficiently accurate description.

"Exactly so, Captain. I'm afraid Captain de la Beche has taken advantage of my good nature. I would like you to bring him before me, so that I can inform him of his many shortcomings."

Sloakum sniffed.

"Where is he now?"

"We do not know, Captain. He appears to have escaped from the Orsonian Empire, so treaty obligations prevent us from pursuing him further. I don't think you will be hindered in the same way."

Sloakum's face creased in what the Lord High Admiral thought might be the vestige of a smile.

"I'll find the scurvy dog, wherever he's skulkin'. Ye want me to string him up?"

The Admiral demurred.

"Any punishment is for me to decide, Captain. I require you only to bring him to me alive."

Sloakum seemed to understand.

"Ye want him trussed up and beaten? We don't charge extra for beatin'. Beatin' comes free," he added.

The Lord High Admiral considered these options. A beating might give him momentary satisfaction, but it might put his recently ennobled state in jeopardy. Who knows how de la Beche would react to such punishment, however deserved? He needed to act a little more circumspectly.

"No. Simply deliver him here unharmed. We will do the rest."

Sloakum grunted.

"What about the rest of his scurvy crew?"

"Do what you like with them, Captain. I have no interest in them whatsoever."

The vestige of a smile became an almost smile.

"Thankee, Admiral. I'll have some of 'em strung up. Nothing my crew likes better than the sight of someone dancin' the hempen jig. The rest I'll put to work, if ye know what I mean."

The Lord High Admiral had only a faint idea of what he meant, but declined to enquire.

"I'm glad we are in agreement, Captain. Now, about the fee. I am prepared to offer you ten thousand Galactic Units of Account, which I am sure you will agree is very generous."

Sloakum shook his head and snorted.

"None of yer funny money, Admiral. I'm done with that. There's only one thing I want payin' in and that's gold."

The Admiral was utterly bemused.

"What do you mean, gold?"

"Gold, Admiral, money ye can get yer teeth into. Money ye can keep to yerself. I keep it in my sea chest and, when I'm about to go to Davy Jones's locker, I'll bury it on a little planet only I know, so no one will ever find it. Ten thousand gold doubloons is my price. Take it or leave it."

The Lord High Admiral recovered quickly from his surprise. Surely among the vast resources for the Orsonian Empire the gold could be found – in doubloons, if necessary, whatever they might be.

"Very well, Captain, if that's what you want. I'll have our lawyers draw up the contract."

Sloakum snorted again.

"None of yer fancy writing, Admiral. I've had enough of it from last time. This time it's just between ye and me. Spit on yer hand and put it up so I can see it, and I'll do the same. Then it's a deal, and, if ye weasel out, things will go badly for ye."

The Admiral overcame his distaste, breathed a barely visible dab of spit on his hand and held it up. On the communicator screen appeared Sloakum's hand, a large gob of yellow-brown sputum sliding down towards his wrist.

***

Civil Servant 21346 was savouring the tumescence stimulated by a particularly salacious article in the *Galactic Inquirer* when the familiar voice echoed from the communicator.

"Civil Servant 21346, come here at once."

As he entered the chamber he saw the Lord High Admiral bent over and fiddling with a communicator screen. After an interval he looked up.

"What do you know about gold, Civil Servant 21346?"

"Gold, Lord High Admiral?"

One of these days, thought the Lord High Admiral, he was going to make Civil Servant 21346 regret his most irritating habit of repeating everything he, the Admiral, said, but that day would have to wait.

"Yes, gold, Civil Servant 21346"

Civil Servant 21346 fiddled with the small communicator on his wrist. After a few seconds he found what he thought he was looking for.

"It's a yellow metal, Lord High Admiral, atomic number 79 which is found ..."

"I don't want you to regurgitate an encyclopedia, Civil Servant 21346. I want to know if we *have* any gold, particularly, what do you call them – doubloons?"

Civil Servant 21346 had no idea what he was talking about, but then that was not an infrequent occurrence.

"Pardon me, Lord High Admiral, but perhaps I could help if you could tell me why you are asking about gold."

The Lord High Admiral could not decide whether this was a genuine attempt to be helpful or Civil Servant 21346's usual display of dumb insolence. He decided to give him the benefit of the doubt.

"I have contracted Captain Sloakum to bring me that arch villain, de la Beche. He has asked to be paid in gold, rather than the usual methods, so we have to find the gold."

Civil Servant 21346 digested this news and thought hard about the least helpful response he could make.

"I'm afraid gold is somewhat outside my area of expertise, Lord High Admiral. The only gold of which I am aware round here is the jewellery worn by ...," he hesitated, "erm ..."

For a brief moment, the Admiral thought that Civil Servant 21346 had gone mad. It was true that he had lavished gifts of gold and jewellery on all his wives and mistresses, as befitting their status as the wives and mistresses of a Lord High Admiral, but there could be no question of that gold being used for paying Sloakum. He could only imagine the outcry there would be if he attempted to take the gold away; he would be courting rebellion if he did the same for the wives and mistresses of other Orsonian high officials.

The same thought had occurred to Civil Servant 21346. He was thinking particularly of a newly-acquired mistress of the Admiral whose luminous beauty and grace had utterly transfixed him when he first saw her. She had adorned herself with bracelets, bangles and earrings of gold that made her all the more alluring, as they shone and sparkled in the early evening light. Normally, she would be far beyond his reach – but suddenly, he saw a glimmer of hope. If the Admiral threatened to take away her jewellery, he would offer to hide it. She in turn would be eager to show her gratitude and he would take her to a secret little boudoir that he would prepare. She would be swept away in ecstasy as he lavished on her all his pent-up ardour. He would luxuriate in her soft, yielding flesh, running his tongue over her pert, erect nipples, sliding his hand up her firm, inviting thighs into ...

"Civil Servant 21346, are you listening to me?"

He snapped back to attention.

"Of course, Lord High Admiral. I was trying to think of any other sources of gold that might be available."

For once, the Admiral decided to take him at his word.

"And are there?"

Civil Servant 21346's face took on an expression of regret, which he was finding harder to maintain as he saw some surprising information appearing on his communicator.

"I'm not sure there are, Lord High Admiral."

The Admiral sat up in exasperation.

"What are you talking about? Gold is just a metal, isn't it? Surely we must have plenty of it on Orson?"

Civil Servant 21346 felt an inward glow of triumph. All those years of avid reading of the *Galactic Enquirer* had given him insight into aspects of the Galaxy entirely unknown to the Admiral.

"It is of course true, as you rightly say, Lord High Admiral, that gold is merely one metal among many, but in some less-developed societies it has a monetary value and so they are eager to acquire it. We on Orson take a more enlightened view."

"Naturally," interrupted the Admiral.

"Naturally, so for us, gold simply has a decorative value and is used mainly in jewellery. However, because these less enlightened societies value it so highly, it is very expensive even on Orson and so only the very highest in society can afford it."

"What about in the rest of the Empire? There must be gold somewhere."

As more information appeared on his communicator, Civil Servant 21346 thought it best to adopt a solemn expression.

"You might remember that one of your predecessors decreed that, in the Empire, only high Orsonian officials and their females were allowed to wear gold. Others had to do with lesser metals like silver. That decree has never been rescinded."

The Admiral inwardly cursed his predecessor and made a note to ensure the removal of any statues or memorials to him.

"Perhaps we may have to ask for a few, er, contributions. I'm sure we can all afford it. How much would we need for Sloakum's price of ten thousand doubloons?"

Civil Servant 21346 peered at his communicator, not quite believing what he was seeing.

"It all depends on what we think a doubloon is worth, Lord High Admiral."

The Admiral was becoming exasperated.

"Stop shilly-shallying, Civil Servant 21346. Just give me a rough idea."

"On some estimates, it is approximately the value of all the gold jewellery on Orson, Lord High Admiral."

The full horror of the situation was beginning to dawn on the Lord High Admiral.

"Are you saying, Civil Servant 21346, that, in order to pay Sloakum, I may have to deprive my wives and mistresses of their jewellery?"

Civil Servant 21346 felt triumph surging, as he tried to maintain his most solemn expression.

"I was not saying that, as such, Lord High Admiral. I was simply pointing out that, as a junior civil servant, I am not aware of all the other sources of gold. Of course, in your exalted position, you must know better."

Normally, the Lord High Admiral would have interpreted this – correctly – as the very quintessence of insolence, but he was far too distracted by the prospect of domestic uproar to notice. Despite his exalted position, he realized that he knew next to nothing about gold, except that it beautifully enhanced the female form, and his females in particular were passionately devoted to it. He felt the first stirrings of panic.

16

Junipa was wrestling with a particularly intricate question of hermeneutics when she heard Orestia's voice emanate from the communicator.

"Junipa, I need to have a word."

By "a word", Orestia always meant something important and she insisted it be face to face, never on the communicator. Junipa reluctantly rose from her chair and made her way to Orestia's office. As she entered, she saw Orestia was studying her communicator screen intently; it was several seconds before she looked up.

"I think we may have a problem."

Junipa looked puzzled.

"About what?"

"Our source on Orson, the one who, in a spirit of sacrifice and devotion to the cause, has remained close, to put it euphemistically, to the appalling High Admiral, has reported that he seems finally to have realized what de la Beche was up to."

Junipa could not suppress a smile.

"That's their problem, surely, not ours. Besides, de la Beche is far to wily to be caught by that pompous idiot."

"That's as may be, but our source informs us that the pompous idiot, as you rightly call him, has engaged another brigand to hunt for de la Beche – a Captain Sloakum. Ever heard of him?"

Junipa's smile turned to laughter.

"The most notorious pirate in the Galaxy! They deserve each other. May they both lose. By the way, have we any idea of where de la Beche is now?"

By the stern look on her face, Junipa could see that Orestia did not share her opinion.

"Little sympathy as I have for either of them, it's not in our interest to have de la Beche in anyone's hands. I understand from another source that he is somewhere on the planet called Libertania, still trying to track down the Kwokkah. We need him at the very least to thwart any attempt by the Orsonians to get their hand on the Kwokkah. If they ever did, then we would have some very big problems. I hardly need remind you that the Orsonians have vowed to crush us and our movement, and they would have the support of every religious zealot in the Galaxy if they did. It's the one thing that they all agree on."

Junipa could only concur, but what was Orestia proposing to do?

"I think we need to fight fire with fire."

"Meaning what?" asked Junipa.

"Meaning our very own pirate."

Junipa gasped in disbelief.

"Maggie Gulliver? You cannot be serious! She's completely uncontrollable. You have no idea what she might do. I thought you said we would never let her out again?"

"Needs must, when the devil drives, as a thousand clerics would doubtless say. We cannot afford to intervene ourselves. That would let the Orsonians know that we have informers in their midst."

Junipa conceded the strength of the argument, but still struggled with the idea that Maggie Gulliver could be the answer to anything. Maggie was female, so the rest of the Galaxy never lost an opportunity to blame the Feminarchs for anything she did. She recalled the time that Gulliver had captured a ship carrying a group of ambassadors on their way to an important Galactic conference and had them all castrated, sending them on their way with a message that they could now concentrate on the important subjects for discussion, rather than what they normally thought about. It had caused uproar throughout the Galaxy, and only strenuous denials of any responsibility by the Feminarchs, and the chronic inability of other federations to act in concert, prevented the Feminarchs from being obliterated. There were countless other wanton acts of piracy, and the Feminarchs, rather reluctantly, concluded that Gulliver had to be stopped. The last straw came when she joined forces with Sloakum to hold up a giant liner that was carrying all sorts of riches, as well as passengers, and sold two hundred women into slavery. Sloakum, true to his nature, had organized a giant orgy to celebrate. They all drank and fornicated themselves senseless and then he and his ship made off with the loot, telling the Feminarchs where Maggie Gulliver could be found. The Feminarchs threw Maggie and crew into their most secure prison, vowing never to let them out. Now, Orestia was proposing to release her. Risky did not come close to describing it.

"Are you sure there's no alternative?" asked Junipa. "What exactly do you imagine Maggie Gulliver could do that would stop Sloakum? She might just as easily attack de la Beche or the Orsonians or anyone else that takes her fancy."

Orestia nodded.

"We know that she still hates Sloakum for what he did, but, even so, we need to take precautions. She will be given strict instructions as to what we expect."

Junipa thought she could see the flaw.

"What if she simply ignores them?"

"That possibility did occur to me, of course, so we will place a control aboard her ship that cannot be deactivated and will render it inoperable if we have reasons to suspect that she is up to no good. We will tell Gulliver that she and her ship will be destroyed if they don't do what we want."

Junipa weighed up the pros and cons of the plan, and decided it might just work.

"We will need to keep a very strict eye on her."

Orestia looked straight at her, her expression one of resolve.

"Quite so, and there is only one person I could entrust with such an important mission – you."

Junipa looked back at Orestia, thunderstruck.

"What? No! I don't think that is a good idea. I have too many duties here, and I need to finish my thesis. Our ideas are on the march. It's most important that we keep up the momentum. Our followers depend on us for ideas and for leadership. My thesis will show them the way forward ..."

Her pleadings did nothing to change Orestia's expression.

"Ideas are all very well, but they must be firmly rooted in practice. Much as I have faith in you, I have thought for some time that you have become a little desk-bound. This will enable you to hone your skills in management and command. If you ever want to aspire to the highest office, you will have to demonstrate that you can do more than turn a persuasive phrase."

***

"Let me at ye, ye pair of taffy-nosed bitches and I'll split ye from starboard to larboard."

Orestia and Junipa gazed at Maggie Gulliver, arms and legs bound to a stout iron chair anchored to the floor, as she writhed, spitting and blaspheming. Her hair, matted, bound and unkempt, fell down over her face, so that her eyes were only partly visible. She was dressed in a rough leather jerkin and trousers, her feet sporting large, hobnailed boots that threw sparks as she banged them on the stone floor.

"I see the years in custody haven't improved your temper, Maggie," said Orestia.

Maggie's response was a cascade of oaths, mostly of an anatomical nature. Orestia's expression remained impassive. Junipa could not suppress a shudder of distaste.

"Now, if you will just control yourself, I think I have a proposal that may allow you your liberty," continued Orestia. "Do you want to hear it?"

Anger and puzzlement contested for dominance on Maggie's face. Eventually, puzzlement won.

"Be quick about it then – and no dissembling. Them 'as tried a lie with Maggie Gulliver soon rued the day their mothers ever spawned 'em."

"Yes, we all know you take a dim view of dishonesty, Maggie," said Orestia, "so I wouldn't dream of attempting to deceive you. Let me get to the point. Do you know of a Captain Sloakum?"

Junipa thought that Maggie's eyes swivelled independently as her face reddened until it was almost crimson.

"Know of him? Why that scurvy spawn of a pox-ridden sea hag tricked me out of the biggest prize I ever took. The devil himself couldn't want for better company. I swore one day I'd have satisfaction of him."

Orestia nodded, displaying just a trace of sympathy.

"Well, this is your chance. Sloakum has been commissioned by the High Admiral of the Orsonian Empire, of whom I expect you have heard and about whom we probably share an opinion, to hunt for a Captain de la Beche. Does that name ring a bell?"

"Wears girlie clothes, talks lah-di-dah and gives out fancy titles to all them he wants to butter up."

Orestia nodded again.

"Yes, I think we are talking about the same person. Your mission is to prevent Sloakum interfering with any actions of de la Beche – at all costs. How you do it is up to you. Is that understood?"

Maggie's expression had by this time regained some composure. She looked down at her shackles.

"I can't do nothing like this."

"Of course," said Orestia, "we are prepared to give you your liberty. In addition we will refurbish your old ship, the *Liberty Belle*, and release your old crew. We only have two provisos. The first is that you will operate under the command of my colleague, Commander Junipa. She will have to agree to any action you take, and if necessary she will be able to give you orders."

Something approximating to a laugh spread across Maggie's features.

"No Captain takes orders from a jumped-up landlubber. If she comes near my ship, I'll have her swinging from the yardarm."

Orestia paused for a moment before she replied.

"Yes, I had anticipated that might be your response. We will place a device on your ship that cannot be deactivated or removed and if for any reason Junipa is prevented from carrying out her duties, it will explode and send you and your crew to the far reaches of the Galaxy. That's the proposal. Take it or leave it."

Junipa watched as conflicting emotions passed over Maggie's face. Eventually, Maggie spoke.

"Damn and blast your eyes, but ye have me where ye want me. Anything is better than this hell hole."

17

The Lord High Admiral of the Orsonian Fleet was feeling a familiar surge of satisfaction as he gazed round at the portrait of his wives, mistresses and children, of whose number he was beginning to lose count. He had just concluded secret negotiations with the Chief of Staff of the Southern Cross Federation, in which they had agreed a non-aggression pact and a most satisfactory distribution of territories. They would exchange a handful of planets of little importance to either and both would annex and share out a goodly portion of the neighbouring Arcturan Empire. The Arcturans could do nothing about it. Their emperor was mad, their treasury bankrupt and their military non-existent. It was also agreed that the Nullarboreans could stew in their religious juices. Neither side really wanted them and they could stay where they were in the Federation.

The Chief of Staff had revealed to him that he was plotting to replace Splenditheran as the head of the Federation. Weak, dithering and unambitious were just some of the shortcomings he perceived in Splenditheran. The agreement with the Orsonians was the dagger he needed. He would show his Ruling Council that he had agreed peace with the Orsonians and that he, as their Commander, could then do what a proper Commander should do and prey upon the weak, dithering and unambitious that could be found in abundance elsewhere in the Galaxy. All was in place. The dagger would be wielded at the next meeting of the Ruling Council.

It was a policy that the Lord High Admiral could only applaud, especially as the Chief of Staff had assured him that there would be rich pickings for the Admiral too. As a bonus, the Chief said he had no interest in the Kwokkah and would assist in the search for de la Beche.

That brought much relief to the Admiral. He had experienced a barrage of abuse when he had suggested to his wives and mistresses that they might, as a patriotic gesture, be prepared to give up a little of their gold for the good of the Empire. Two of his wives, Third and Fourth Lady High Admirals, had not only refused point blank, but had detailed in the most graphic terms the limitations of his love-making techniques and more than hinted that they had better offers elsewhere from parties who would never be so mean as to suggest that they part with their beloved jewellery. The combined forces of the Southern Cross and the Orsonians were sure to be able to find de la Beche. He had no further need of Sloakum – and so no need for gold. He would convey the good news to his wives and mistresses. They would be overwhelmed with gratitude – and gratitude, as is well known, is the precursor to libidinousness. As for the two who questioned his virility, he would show them what a Lord High Admiral was made of.

There was only one small cloud on the horizon – how to tell Sloakum that his services were no longer required? The Admiral thought that he would not be best pleased to hear the news and then, on thinking a little more, that Sloakum was not best pleased about anything, but this was likely to irk him more than most things. In the circumstances, he thought it would be unseemly for a Lord High Admiral to be involved in a vulgar squabble. The decision would best be conveyed by an underling, and he had a specific underling in mind. Dumb insolence would be no use this time.

"Civil Servant 21346, come in here at once."

The civil servant entered with what, if the Admiral had been taking any notice, he would have thought was a suspiciously upbeat demeanour. However, the Admiral had other things on his mind.

"Civil Servant 21346, I am going to entrust you with a most delicate task. Only you and I will know about it. I trust that you can keep everything secret."

Civil Servant 21346 was taken aback. It was the first time that the Lord High Admiral had addressed him in terms other than barely-concealed contempt. He blushed.

"Of course, Lord High Admiral. You can rely on me."

The Admiral smiled inwardly. Concealment of contempt made the contempt all the sweeter. He liked being contemptuous. What was the point of being a Lord High Admiral if you couldn't be contemptuous of your inferiors?

"Civil Servant 21346, for the time being this will go no further than this room. You will remain here to perform your duties. On the Most Secret part of our system, you will find headings of agreement that I have concluded with a representative of the Southern Cross Federation."

Civil Servant 21346 could not prevent an involuntary drawing in of breath. The Admiral nodded.

"As I said, this is most delicate, as well as most secret. I want you to draw up a legal treaty based on those headings. You will see that, as a result of the agreement, we will no longer be in dispute with the Federation over certain territories and will have their full support in apprehending the renegade de la Beche. As a consequence, we no longer have need of the services of Captain Sloakum. You will contact Captain Sloakum and tell him of our decision. You can, of course, offer him compensation, but on no account must gold be mentioned. Is that clear? On no account."

What was clear to Civil Servant 21346 was that he was being pitched into some very dirty work indeed. Worse, plans he had been making looked as if they might come to nothing. He needed to know more. The best strategy was to play things very straight. That always annoyed the Admiral and he might reveal more than he intended.

"Quite clear, Lord High Admiral. Are the details of Captain Sloakum's contract on the system as well?"

The Admiral glared at the civil servant. Up to his usual tricks. Quite incorrigible.

"It was a gentlemen's agreement, Civil Servant 21346."

The civil servant could only wonder at the notion of a gentlemen's agreement with Sloakum, but, again, kept things straight.

"I'm sure it was, Lord High Admiral, but what about the Termination Clause?"

The Admiral's impatience quotient was beginning to rise.

"The Termination Clause?"

"Yes. I need to know details, so I can calculate how much compensation Captain Sloakum would be due. I assume there is a Termination Clause?"

The Admiral's glare increased in intensity. He knew full well that Civil Servant 21346 knew full well that there was no Termination Clause, or indeed clauses of any sort. He decided to brazen things out and waved a hand dismissively.

"Details, details, Civil Servant 21346. Captain Sloakum is not a details person. His sort never is. Just offer him enough to go away."

The civil servant's anxiety was mounting. He needed to know how much time he had.

"When will the treaty come into operation, Lord High Admiral?"

The Admiral hesitated, unsure of how much to divulge.

"It depends on certain developments in the Southern Cross Federation, Civil Servant 21346. You do not need to know the details. Get on with the task I have given you."

18

Desperation was beginning to overwhelm Civil Servant 21346. Everything he had planned for – everything he had hoped for – was threatening to fall apart. Success had been so near he could almost taste it. Lust and revenge, the twin driving forces of his being, were to come together in one delicious, triumphant package. Now, all could turn to dust.

For ages he had been attempting to woo one of the Admiral's mistresses. She was young, lithe, raven-haired and almost indescribably beautiful. He was utterly besotted and made a habit of always being the first to offer his services when the Admiral wanted an escort for his harem on any trips they made. By smiles, compliments and little gestures he hoped to attract her attention. At first, she appeared to take little notice of him, beyond the occasional fluttering of eyelashes. Undeterred, he persisted. He spent much of his meagre salary on his appearance – on clothes, hair and grooming. He forced himself to learn reams of love poetry that he hoped would convince her of his fine manners and even finer mind. Gradually, he convinced himself that he was succeeding. They exchanged the occasional word and she was amused – or at least appeared to be amused – when he quoted a particularly apposite line of poetry. Then, all of a sudden, things changed.

She was a particular favourite of the Admiral, who had appointed her *Maîtresse en titre,* to the chagrin of his other mistresses, and had showered her with gifts of gold and jewellery. Now he had suggested that she give some of them back, but refused to say why. At first she had thought of withholding her favours, but realized that the Admiral would give her position to another of his mistresses. So she demurred, sweet-talking the Admiral into conceding that she would be the very last to have to give up her gold and then only if it was absolutely necessary. Naturally, she did not believe a word he said, so she began looking for ways that she might keep her precious possessions. That was when Civil Servant 21346 saw his chance.

Among his tasks was arranging collection of gold to pay Sloakum, a task with which he was having very little success. Gold was in very short supply elsewhere in the Orsonian Empire, and deranged fury considerably understated the resentment felt by the Orsonian female elite when asked to part with any of their treasures. When, during an outing, she made her feelings clear, Civil Servant 21346 expressed sympathy and, for the first time, she began a conversation with him. It turned out that she was the daughter of the leader of a distant planet of the Empire. The Admiral made a habit of collecting wives and mistresses from far-flung parts of the Empire in order to ensure their allegiance. Her father had been against her becoming one of the Admiral's mistresses, but she had insisted, dazzled by the prospect of Planet Orson. If the Admiral persisted in taking her gold, she might go back to her father. She wasn't afraid of any Admiral.

Civil Servant 21346 found an idea beginning to form itself. He would suggest that she did allow the Admiral to take her gold, but he, Civil Servant 21346, with his access to its collection, would keep it aside. At a suitable time, they could both escape with her gold to her father's planet, where they would be safe. He used the word 'elope' to himself, but thought it might be a little premature to mention it to her. However, he was convinced that she was bound to be overcome by his gallantry and daring and fall madly in love with him. He almost swooned with desire and elation at the prospect.

Now, with no need for Sloakum, there was no need for gold and no need for elopement. It was too much to bear. All his anger and resentment and jealousy of the Admiral boiled over. He tried hard to think of something – anything – that could distract him from his anguish, and found himself looking at the heads of agreement between the Admiral and the Southern Cross Federation. What he saw gave him just a flicker of hope.

Nothing was stated explicitly, but Civil Servant 21346 had enough experience of the Admiral's ways to realize that a very devious game was being played. It seemed that there was a plot against Splenditheran, the Commander of the Southern Cross Federation, and a secret agreement between the Southern Cross and the Orsonians to exchange planets. Worse, between them they proposed to carve up the Arcturan Empire. Who knew what the consequences of that would be, once other parts of the Galaxy heard about it? Worst of all, of course, was the Sloakum business. It was clear that everything depended on the ousting of Splenditheran. There was still time. The Agreement had not been signed; the Council had not met. If Splenditheran could be tipped off, then the whole plot might collapse.

How to do it? Direct communication was out of the question. Even if it were possible, all communications were monitored and, if Civil Servant 21346 tried, he would very quickly find himself in an execution pod. Then an idea occurred to him – what about de la Beche? If he could be told, then he could tell Splenditheran. But again, any attempt to contact de la Beche, given his treachery, would mean instant execution. He was about to despair, when suddenly he saw a way – do it by tender.

His department was constantly sending out tenders for all sorts of services. Nobody but those involved paid any attention to them. Who wants to read a tender? All he needed to do was to disguise the message in a tender document and make sure it reached de la Beche. Simple? No, it wasn't, but that wasn't going to stop him trying. He began to draw up the document. Despite all his experience of mind-numbing bureaucratic drafting, he found it one of the hardest things he had ever done. Eventually he managed to craft something.

Notice of Tender

Project: Replacement of the existing control system of the AustraloCrux Corporation following proposal of joint venture with OE Inc. and development of newly-acquired properties.

Project Location; Headquarters of the AustraloCrux Corporation.

Timescale: Imminent.

Specification: The proposed joint venture between AustraloCrux Corporation and OE Inc. will involve:

- Combining their complementary skills and capabilities
- Expansion into wholly new areas of activity. This will involve replacement of the outdated control system at AutraloCrux Corporation with a new and dynamic system capable of maximizing the exciting opportunities that the joint venture will offer.

Organizations with sufficient expertise and capability who wish to participate should reply in strictest confidence to the Chief Operating Officer of the AustraloCrux Corporation.

Civil Servant 21346 looked doubtfully at what he had written. Was it too vague? Would anyone reading it understand what it meant? On the other hand, if he made it any more specific, he might be caught. It was the best he could do. Who to send it to? De la Beche, obviously, but not just to him. He drew up a list of deadbeat and defunct organizations that he knew would not even bother to read the document, let alone respond, inserted the *Bountiful*'s address discreetly among them, and sent it off. After that was only the waiting.

19

The Arcturan Empire

The Arcturan Empire is unique in the Galaxy in that its constitution decrees that the ruling monarch must always display some form of insanity. Accepted disorders include megalomania, narcissism, psychoses and all types of dementia. Fortunately, the ruling family has historically been fecund and changes – or defects, depending on your point of view – in its genetic inheritance have meant that there has never been any shortage of suitable candidates.

Traditionally, Arcturan monarchs have concentrated on amassing as much wealth as possible and building enormous palaces on their home planet, Arctura, in the most florid style, adorned by artworks of grandiose proportions and simpering sentimentality. They never ventured outside their palaces and never met any of their subjects, other than their palace servants. Instead, they believed that the duty of monarchs was to indulge themselves in all manner of vices and eccentricities, the more excessive the better. Their decrees were almost always arbitrary and often incomprehensible, and were therefore ignored by the populace. Some rules, however, are observed. Being a banker, accountant, bond-dealer or stockbroker is a capital offence. That is to ensure that any currency introduced is instantly debauched, inflation is infinite, unlimited credit is always available and no debt is ever repaid. Consequently, the economy ticks along nicely and most Arcturans admit that they have never had it so good.

Beyond these fiscal observances, there are few if any rules in Arcturan society. All forms of bars, casinos, bordellos, brothels, cat-houses, drug-dens and burlesque joints abound, a magnet for many in the rest of the Galaxy.

Neighbouring polities have often cast covetous eyes on the Arcturan Empire, but have always held back from any action, partly because they feared the wrath of others with similar ambitions and also because they were afraid that their own populace might become infected with Arcturan attitudes. So, as anyone who visits will find, the Arcturan mantra is always "The party goes on."

An extract from 'Lonely Planets', *the memoirs of Gaudi Brandeschi, interstellar traveller and troubadour. The book is banned in all Galactic jurisdictions on grounds ranging from criminal libel, sedition, blasphemy and salacious recitation to lèse-majesté. A great number of arrest warrants for Brandeschi are extant. His current whereabouts are unknown.*

Captain Sloakum looked upon the unlovely faces of his crew with a familiar mixture of contempt and hatred. Gizzard slittin' was almost too good for them. They gazed back with feelings that were more than reciprocated. The *Rum, Sodomy and the Lash* was safely parked in orbit around the Arcturan home star, and Sloakum and his crew had descended in the ship's cutter to the capital, Baccanorgia. They were going ashore to prime themselves for the next job, the hunt for de la Beche. Sloakum gave them his customary piece of mind.

"I knows what ye're all thinking. Ye all think ye're never coming back. Ye think ye'll find another ship's captain stupid enough to take ye on, or some brainless floozie that'll cosset yer useless carcass for the rest of yer miserable life. But I knows better. When ye've been kicked out of every public house in this town, when every gambling-den and shebeen has slammed the door in yer face and, when the grasping strumpets round here have taken yer last penny-piece, ye'll come crawling back, because no one else will have ye. And when ye do ye had better have a note from a quack that says he's cured ye of whatever pox or pestilence ye've caught while ye've been here, or I'll have yer privates dangling from the yardarm. Now get out of my sight before I give ye all a taste of my cutlass."

There was a low, grumbling sound from the crew before they began to slope off. As they descended the gangplank of the cutter, their mood visibly lightened. By the time they reached solid ground their pace had quickened to a brisk walk, almost a trot, as they lit out for the myriad bars and cat-houses that lined the outskirts of the Arcturan spaceport. Sloakum watched them disappear, then hailed a passing cab. As they started, he roundly cursed the cabbie, who had unwisely attempted to engage him in conversation, and sat back in silence as they drove to his destination.

The *Toxic Toad* was notorious even by the standard of Arcturan drinking dens. It attracted a clientele that proudly considered themselves the lowest and worst in the Galaxy. They came in a spirit of general debauchery to enjoy the Arcturan delights and to compare exploits, often with the intention of depriving their companions of their ill-gotten gains. The conversations often turned violent and occasionally murderous; and so the landlord had an arrangement with the local constabulary for the discreet disposal of corpses in such situations.

As Sloakum entered, he saw the familiar notice:

> **Detectors are in operation. All weapons must be left at the door.**

Slapping, tickling or other molestation of staff is forbidden, unless the required deposit is paid in advance.

Customers who wish to engage in physical altercations of any kind must do so in the ring outside. All such actions at own risk.

This was an atmosphere that Sloakum found entirely congenial. He was considered an honoured guest of the establishment. His prowess in the slitting of gizzards was acknowledged with great respect, to the point that he was allowed to bring his cutlass into the bar. He looked forward to quaffing quantities of ale, devouring several of his favourite steaks and, as a bonus, if things went well, enjoying a little blood-letting.

Things did begin well. The ale flowed, an extra barrel was laid on, and several of the other drinkers insisted on buying a flagon for Sloakum to show their esteem. He was on his third steak when there was a commotion. Sloakum looked up from his plate and for a moment could not believe his eyes.

A figure had appeared in the doorway. A figure dressed all in leather – jerkin, trousers and boots – with long, bedraggled hair topped with a wide-brimmed hat bedecked with equally bedraggled flowers. A figure that he thought he would never see again.

All eyes in the *Toxic Toad* turned towards the door. For several seconds, the figure surveyed the room and then let out a roar of recognition.

"Jonah Sloakum! Of all the bars on all the planets in all the Galaxy, I knew I'd find ye in this one. And I see ye're keeping yer usual company with the meanest, scurvyest bilge rats that ever crawled."

Sloakum continued chewing on his steak, then downed half a flagon of ale before answering.

"Takes one to know one, Maggie."

Maggie Gulliver tossed her head angrily and pulled out a metal implement from her waistband.

"Got ye at last, Jonah Sloakum, after all yer lyin' and cheatin'. Ye cheated me out of the biggest prize I ever had, the *Golden Horn*, worth an emperor's ransom, it was. Now I'm going to blow ye to hell. Prepare to breathe yer last."

Sloakum let out a great bellow of a laugh and pulled out his cutlass.

"Ye and whose army Maggie? I should have had ye strung up last time I clapped eyes on ye, but I suppose I'll have to do the job now. Are ye going to slap me in the face with that bit of tin ye have in yer hand? If ye try, I'll slit ye from stern to bowsprit with this."

Sloakum saw Maggie's finger jerk on the implement and heard a loud bang as something hot whizzed by his face. Startled, he jumped back. There was a gasp of astonishment from the others in the bar, and the landlord gave a yell.

"What the devil was that? Why wasn't it detected? Get her out of here!"

Maggie waved the implement in the air.

"Nobody move. This is a pistol, a proper weapon. None of yer fancy rays or blasters, which is why yer detectors didn't pick it up. It's an old timer and shoots lead. Any of ye that gets a belly full of lead will have more than guts ache, I can tell ye."

Her eyes narrowed as she looked at Sloakum.

"Now, Jonah Sloakum, on yer knees. I want to hear ye beg before I finish ye off."

Sloakum gave a snort.

"I kneel for no one, Maggie Gulliver."

"Ye'll kneel if I shoot ye in the leg. The choice is your'n."

Sloakum looked round the bar, but saw that no help would be forthcoming. He sank slowly to his knees, still clutching his cutlass.

"Shoot and be damned, Maggie Gulliver. Ye'll get no more out of me."

She gave a mirthless laugh.

"Well, I won't get back what ye cheated me out of, that's for certain. Ye and that scurvy bunch of vermin ye call a crew will have long since pissed and whored it away."

Sloakum stared back at her, as if contemplating something.

"Don't be so sure, Maggie. Maybe I could make it up to ye."

The laugh was louder, but just as mirthless.

"I never had ye marked down as a joker, Jonah Sloakum. Where'd that come from?"

It was Sloakum's turn to give a sort of laugh.

"Let's see if I'm joking, Maggie. Maybe ye could tell us how ye got out. I thought those girlies had ye in irons for ever."

"They let me out so I could do for ye, Jonah Sloakum. And so here I am."

Sloakum's grizzled face displayed an expression akin to puzzlement.

"Why would they want done with me?"

This time Maggie's roar of laughter was real.

"Maybe they just joined the rest of the Galaxy in wanting yer guts."

Sloakum shook his head.

"Nay, Maggie. That don't fool me. They had to have a reason."

Maggie smirked.

"I suppose I might as well let ye know before I let ye have it. They want ye gone because they heard that dawcock of an Orsonian admiral wants ye to fetch him nancy boy de la Beche, and they don't want him fetched. They thought it would give me the greatest pleasure to do for ye – and they were right."

Sloakum nodded.

"They're right about de la Beche. The devil only knows why those Orsonians want him, but don't give me any guff that they just let you out. They're keeping their eyes on ye, aren't they?"

"Maybe they are and maybe they aren't, but where ye're going ye won't be caring."

"Thought as much. They won't let ye do anything they don't want. And what about that ramshackle tub of your'n – did they let ye have that too?"

Maggie gave him her fiercest stare.

"What's it to you?"

"It was only good for the breaker's yard, last time I looked. Ye must be running out of string to keep its bits together by now. What ye need is a real fighting ship."

Maggie gave another snort.

"What, like your'n?"

Sloakum almost smiled.

"No finer fighting ship anywhere than the *Rum, Sodomy and the Lash*, Maggie. Now, what if I make ye an offer? What would ye say to some gold?"

Maggie stared at him with an expression of disbelief.

"What do ye know about gold, Jonah Sloakum?"

Sloakum's face creased further.

"I know it's real money, Maggie, not paper stuff or funny numbers on screens. It's money that ye can hold in the palm of yer hand and bite with yer teeth. It's money that ye can spend anywhere and no questions asked."

Maggie added dismissal to her disbelief.

"And where would ye get gold, Jonah Sloakum?"

Sloakum raised his cutlass hand and banged on the table.

"From the very dawcock ye mentioned, the fat tub of lard that calls himself Lord High Admiral. I bring him de la Beche, all trussed up like a turkey, and he pays me in gold doubloons. What would ye say to sailing with me and having yerself a share of that gold?"

Maggie stared at him, unable to decide whether he was serious.

"Why should I sail with ye, Jonah Sloakum? I have my own ship and crew."

Now it was Sloakum's turn to be dismissive.

"Call that sailing, Maggie? Ye're just an errand girl. Ye do fer me, and the girlies'll have no use for ye after that. They'll have ye and yer crew dancing the hempen jig before ye can say Davy Jones Locker."

Maggie turned this over in her mind. The more she thought, the more she realized, very reluctantly, that Sloakum might be right. Even more thought began to make the prospect of gold seem attractive.

"If I sail with ye, would ye want my crew as well?"

Sloakum almost exploded at the thought. Women aboard ship were the very devil.

"Nay, Maggie. Just ye. Ye and me know how to deal with a crew. The harder ye treat 'em, the quicker they shape up."

Maggie had to admit to a feeling of relief. The years of incarceration had done nothing to improve the performance or the temper of her crew. She would let them go hang, and most of them probably would. She turned to a more important question.

"About this gold, Jonah Sloakum. How much is the Admiral paying ye?"

Sloakum cleared his throat and pursed his lips.

"Five thousand gold doubloons."

Maggie knew he was lying, but didn't know by how much.

"I'll take half. "

Sloakum spluttered indignantly

"Ye'll do no such thing. The crew gets a fifth, ye can have a fifth and rest is mine. Take it or leave it."

Maggie smiled sardonically.

"Ye're in no position to give me last chances, Jonah Sloakum. I'll give ye one. Two thousand or I blast ye to Hell. What's it to be?"

For long seconds, Sloakum said nothing. Finally, he spoke.

"Ye win Maggie. Two thousand it is."

Maggie gave him a long look.

"Let's see ye make the Pirate Promise, Jonah Sloakum. Then I might believe ye."

Sloakum grimaced and then nodded. Maggie put the pistol back in her belt. They both spat in their palms and then shook hands. The deal was sealed. The one thing never done was to break the Pirate Promise.

20

Jim returned to the Bridge from showing Bosun Bones and the Bold Deceiver the delights of the *Bountiful*'s kitchen to find de la Beche, Doctor Culpepper and Mister Betelgeuse gathered round a console.

"So what does *Galactopedia* tell us about Roy Pesshe?" asked de la Beche.

"It is rather curious, Captain," replied Mister Betelgeuse. "Querying 'Roy Pesshe' returns 'see Pesshe, Roy' and querying 'Pesshe, Roy' returns 'see Roy Pesshe'. It would seem that whatever information the system contains is being withheld."

De la Beche sighed.

"What about poor mad Mandragore? Has he anything to say?"

Mister Betelgeuse nodded.

"I have consulted the *Principia Ontologica*, which, as you imply, can be somewhat eccentric in its views, and I did find one mention":

The Information Bound

Following on from the work of De'neev and Strengupan, Danikil, in *The Thermodynamic Foundations of Information*, showed that at the De'neev maximum, the information system can be considered closed – any additional information does not add to the integrated total. Danikil showed further that for any element within the system to achieve cognitive hegemony it must attain a cognition level at least two orders of magnitude higher than any other element in the system. Since, in any adiabatic isolated system, information flows from knowledge towards ignorance, it is impossible to maintain hegemony without barriers to information flow. Furthermore, in order to ensure that hegemony is permanent and cannot be challenged, it is necessary not only to eliminate information flow, but also to erase all history that might reveal any such information existed.

The Panalecton is the exemplar of Danikil's work. It maintains an information level several orders of magnitude higher than any other by employing a number of techniques:

- Erasing all knowledge of the evolution of sentient races and the history of their spread throughout the Galaxy.
- Directing aspirations for explanation of reality into religion, usually of a revelatory monotheistic type, where sacred texts reveal a god's desire for unreflective worship.
- Inculcating in each sentient race its own origin myth and the belief that it is uniquely favoured by a deity jealous of its prerogatives and antagonistic to any challenge.
- Ensuring constant low-level conflicts between competing domains to preoccupy ruling elites, encourage martial attitudes and discourage the development of intellectual enquiry.
- Maintaining a stable level of technology, preventing further development and not allowing any race or organization to gain a significant technical advantage over any other.
- Carefully filtering such information as it allows to be disseminated, mostly through its main outlet *Galactopedia*, so that it appears to be rigorous and objective, but in reality supports the objectives of the Panalecton.

> There have been occasional reports of challenges to the Panalecton in the form of repositories of information, but most have turned out to be illusory. The most persistent reports are of an entity called Roy Pesshe. Quite what Roy Pesshe is has never been adequately explained, and its existence must be considered questionable.

De la Beche turned to Mister Betelgeuse.

"Is that all?"

"I'm afraid so, Captain. I have trawled through all our sources of information and that is the only mention of Roy Pesshe that I can find."

De la Beche was about to reply when Gobby, the comms operator, interrupted.

"Sorry, Captain, I've got something here that I don't know what to make of. Perhaps you should take a look at it?"

He showed it to de la Beche, who shook his head dismissively.

"It's just a tender document or something. And it's from the Orsonians of all people. Why are you bothering me with it?"

Gobby persisted.

"It doesn't seem to make sense, Captain, and why are they sending it to us?"

De la Beche waved a hand.

"In my experience, very little from the Orsonians makes sense. Mr Betelgeuse, perhaps you could take a look and then tell Gobby he's worrying his pretty head over nothing."

Mister Betelgeuse perused the message. Jim watched and thought he saw the semblance of a frown on his normally impassive features.

"It may be nothing, Captain, but, on the other hand, there may be a message contained in it. It mentions the AustraloCrux Corporation. AustraloCrux could be an old form of Southern Cross."

"So what if it did, Mister Betelgeuse?"

Mister Betelgeuse continued examining the tender.

"OE Inc. might be the Orsonian Empire. It talks about a new joint venture between them and the replacement of the 'outdated control system' of the AustraloCrux Corporation. Is this hinting at some sort of secret pact between them to join forces?"

De la Beche looked sceptical.

"That doesn't make sense. We know Splenditheran absolutely distrusts the Orsonians because of the Nullarborean business. That's why he wants us to find the Kwokkah."

"True, Captain, but could the 'outdated control system' be Commander Splenditheran? This message could be informing us of a plot to oust him and suggesting we contact him. Look at the last line – 'reply in strictest confidence to the Chief Operating Officer of the AustraloCrux Corporation'. The Chief Operating Office of the Southern Cross Federation is not Commander Splenditheran, it is the Chief of Staff."

De la Beche was unconvinced.

"I'm rather surprised at you, Mister Betelgeuse. That seems very fanciful. Who on Orson would want to tip us off about a plot against Splenditheran, and why would they do it like that?"

Mister Betelgeuse's tone of voice was unchanged as he responded.

"I have no answer to your first question, Captain, but I would suggest that whoever sent it was attempting to disguise it so that it would not be detected. That would indicate that they are quite close to the central Orsonian command. On the other hand, it may simply be a tender, although a rather curious one. Perhaps we could check by investigating the corporations mentioned?"

De la Beche shrugged.

"I suppose we could, providing it doesn't take too long."

Jim watched as Mister Betelgeuse studied a terminal.

"There appears to be no mention in any Orsonian business directory of an AustraloCrux Corporation, Captain, and nothing that would match the description OE Inc. that corresponds to what is mentioned in the tender document, nor anything similar in Southern Cross Federation directories."

De la Beche frowned.

"Maybe there is something to it after all? If Splenditheran goes, then we could kiss goodbye to our fee. I think I should have a word with him, but it is going to be tricky. Who knows who else might be listening in?"

De la Beche sat back in his chair and pondered for several minutes. The others watched, saying nothing. Eventually, he spoke.

"Is the secure channel that Splenditheran set up still working?"

"We haven't deactivated it," said Gobby. "I don't know whether they have."

"Let's try it."

Jim saw Gobby go over to another console and manipulate the controls. For perhaps a minute nothing seemed to be happening, then suddenly the face of a clearly surprised Splenditheran appeared on a screen.

"Captain de la Beche, you have news for me?"

"We do, darling, though not perhaps of the sort you were expecting. This is a matter of some delicacy. Can I ask if you are alone?"

Splenditheran's surprise increased.

"What do you mean – alone?"

"Well, can anyone else overhear this conversation?"

"Certainly not."

"Good, because we have reason to believe that someone is plotting to get rid of you."

Splenditheran's face took on an expression that appeared to be a mixture of astonishment and scorn.

"I don't believe that for a minute, Captain. I can assure you that I have the full support of our Ruling Council."

"I do hope you're right, but we have received a tip-off that someone on your side is planning to do a deal with the Orsonians and replace you."

Splenditheran's expression hardly changed.

"What sort of tip-off?"

"Well, it came in a rather unusual form: a tender document."

"A what? Captain, this is becoming less believable by the second."

De la Beche nodded sympathetically.

"I quite understand, darling. We were very doubtful ourselves at first, but we've made a few enquiries and we think it may be genuine. I would advise you to watch your back. One can't be too careful these days, in my experience."

"Yes, well your experience is very different from mine, as I understand. I have the full confidence of my colleagues on the Ruling Council and they have mine. I think we should leave it at that, Captain."

His face disappeared from the screen.

21

"What do you mean 'gone'?"

Orestia was looking sternly at a crestfallen Junipa, whose face was betraying the first signs of panic.

"Just that – gone. She sent an expletive-laden message to her crew, telling them that they could get lost. She had had a better offer."

Junipa's panic rose another notch, as the normally imperturbable Orestia slammed her hand down on the desk.

"Better offer! What do you mean better offer? Who would make any sort of offer to Maggie Gulliver? She's wanted in every jurisdiction in the Galaxy. The only offer she's ever likely to get is a quick trip to an execution pod."

Junipa could only agree.

"It does seem extraordinary. I can't think of anyone or any thing that would want her."

She was trying to come up with a tactful way of reminding Orestia that it was her idea to release Maggie in the first place, when Orestia spoke.

"Where is her ship now?"

Junipa consulted a screen.

"Still in orbit round Arctura. We have immobilized it. It can't go anywhere, unless we let it."

"What was she doing there?"

"Maggie claimed that it was the best place to find out anything about Sloakum. You know what it's like. The place is crawling with low-lifes and scumbags of every description. Maggie said that one of them might know where Sloakum was."

"And did they?"

"We don't know. That was the last we heard from her."

Orestia shook her head.

"What a mess. We had better cut our losses. Get the ship back here, and lock up the crew. And let's find Maggie, and do the same to her. We can't have her on the loose. There's no knowing the trouble she might cause."

"How are we going to do that?"

Orestia's expression became sterner still.

"How are *you* going to do it? I put you in charge of making sure Maggie toed the line, and look what happened. It's your mess, so you have to clear it up. I suggest you go straight to Arctura, and see what you can find out."

***

Junipa felt the glare of a sun whiter and larger than the one she was used to on her face. Even with dark glasses, she had to shield her eyes. She had emerged from the Arcturan spaceport and stood at the side of a wide road, wondering what she should do next. She had hoped to enlist the support of local Feminarch adherents, but had been quickly disabused of the idea by the Head of Secret Networks. "Absolutely unreliable. Too interested in having a good time. They get drunk and blab about everything."

She had dressed as she thought appropriately in a well-tailored light grey jacket and trousers, but looking around, she realized she would stand out in any crowd. The males appeared to wear mostly ill-fitting singlets and shorts, while the females wore far too little and flaunted as much flesh as possible. Across the road was an apparently endless vista of establishments claiming to cater for every imaginable vice and fancy. The entire place was clearly beyond redemption.

As she stood, a large taxi, garish with advertisements for premises of doubtful repute, pulled up. The driver yelled out the window, "Going into town?"

She hesitated, repelled by the adverts, but then decided to get in. If Maggie Gulliver had come to Arctura, she would have made straight for the dens of iniquity that infested Baccanorgia, and this driver looked as if he knew where they were.

The driver was cheerful, rotund and bald, everything she hated in a male. He struck up conversation immediately.

"Just finished my shift. Off home now for a shower, shave and a shit, and then out on the town for a bit of you know what, if you get what I mean."

Junipa felt an involuntary shudder travel down her spine.

"I don't believe I do."

The driver shot her a glance and gave a half chuckle.

"Oops. I shouldn't have said that, should I?"

Junipa saw no point in hiding her reaction.

"No, you shouldn't."

The driver chuckled again.

"You don't look like the sort of female we usually get round here."

Junipa felt another shudder.

"Really? What are the usual 'sort'?"

"Well they're all slags round here, aren't they? All on one game or another. I can see you're different. You've got a bit of class."

Junipa decided that she would not dignify his remarks with a response. She sat stiffly upright, staring straight ahead. The driver gave her another glance.

"Oops, again. I shouldn't have said that either, should I?"

Junipa remained staring silently ahead. The driver tried another tack.

"Let's talk about something else. What are you like on philosophy?"

Junipa was so surprised by his question that she answered before she could stop herself.

"Philosophy?"

"Yeah, philosophy. You know – all that 'what's it all about' stuff. I had that Ostallbert Mulbankian in the back of the cab the other day. He's a famous philosopher. You must have heard of him. So I said to him, 'What's it all about then, Osto?'"

Junipa thought she had heard that one.

"You're going to say that he couldn't tell you."

The driver looked surprised.

"No, no, he could tell me alright. He wouldn't stop telling me all the way into town. Didn't understand a word of it. I had brain-ache for a week after. Do you understand any of it?"

Junipa thought it was best to humour him, if she was to get any information from him that might be useful in finding Maggie Gulliver.

"As a matter of fact, I do. I am writing a dissertation on the hermeneutics of gender that contains many novel philosophical ideas."

The driver seemed impressed.

"Way to go, lady. Gender, that's sex isn't it? Is it mucky?"

Junipa raised her eyes to the heavens in exasperation. There was no point in idle conversation with this person. Maybe she should try a direct question.

"Look, I'm trying to track down someone I once knew. Have you ever heard of someone called Maggie Gulliver?"

The driver gave it some thought and then shook his head.

"Don't think I do. I know a lot of the girls in town. Maybe they would know her. We could ask them if you like?"

"I don't think so. She's not that sort of 'girl'."

For a few moments Junipa was silent and then another idea occurred to her.

"What about someone called Sloakum? Have you heard of him?"

The driver chortled.

"Are you talking about Captain Sloakum? We all know him. What a character! He's a regular round these parts. He was here the other day, but he's gone now. One of his crew tried to get me to give him a ride to catch his ferry, only he was skint. I had to kick him out of the cab."

Junipa considered this a lead worth pursuing.

"Are you sure he's not here now?"

"Definitely. We always know when Captain Sloakum's in town."

"When is he likely to be back?"

"Couldn't say, lady. Captain Sloakum is his own man. He don't run to no timetable."

If Sloakum was in town, then Maggie must have been hot on his trail. Where would she go to find him?

"Is there anywhere that Sloakum would usually go when he is here?"

The driver nodded vigorously.

"You're talking about the *Toad*, the *Toxic Toad*. It's a joint downtown. It's his favourite spot. Always goes there when he comes to town."

"Take me there."

The driver looked at her with a very doubtful expression.

"You don't want to go there, lady. It's not for the likes of you."

Junipa turned to him.

"I insist. Take me there. I'll make it worth your while."

The driver shrugged.

"OK, lady. You're the boss. But don't say I didn't warn you. You won't like it."

***

Junipa ignored the louring mask of an amphibian over the entrance and pushed open the door of the *Toxic Toad*. Inside the ambience was close, sweaty and grotesquely male. The lighting was low, but along the walls she could make out pictures of males in various swaggering poses, flaunting weapons, fists or their bare torsos. The clientele was entirely male, some of them comatose, stretched out on chairs or benches, as lightly-clad serving maids stepped over and around them, delivering drinks and food.

As Junipa went towards the bar, she felt a hand on her thigh moving towards her crotch. She made a quick chopping motion with her right hand. It was a move she had practised many times in martial arts, and it was guaranteed to break at least two fingers. There was a loud yelp of pain. Customers turned their heads to see what had happened and several of them started sniggering. She saw the barman look up and point.

"Oi, Dendrick, I've told you about that before. You never pay the fondling charge anyway, and now look what you get."

She turned round to see a figure, presumably Dendrick, slumped over a table, his face contorted with pain. She gave him a sardonic smile and went to the bar. The barman looked her over before speaking.

"What can I get you? A port and lemon? A nice little white wine?"

Junipa stared back at him.

"A fruit juice."

The barman appeared surprised.

"We don't get asked for that very often. We should have some, somewhere." He rummaged under the bar, pulled out a bottle and brushed dust off it. "Here we are. I knew we had some."

As he was pouring, a tall, gangly figure dressed in a loud check jacket approached and put his arm round Junipa; his hand moved up towards her breast.

"What have we here, then? You never told me about this little poppet, Zacko," he said to the barman and then, pushing his face close to Junipa's, "I bet you're looking for a real man, aren't you, darling, someone who can show you … argh…."

He had collapsed writhing on the floor, clutching his crotch, gasping for breath.

The barman nodded appreciatively at Junipa.

"That was quick. I didn't even see it."

The figure on the floor was spitting with fury.

"You're not going to let her get away with this, Zacko, are you?"

The barman gave a half smile.

"Course I am, Furgood. The lady bought a drink. When's the last time you paid for anything here? If you're not out of here pronto, you'll lose what's left of your todger to my boot. I heard it's not much use to you anyway. Megsi here," he said, nodding towards one of the servers, "tells me you tried it on with her last week and it was about as much use as a string screwdriver."

Furgood rose unsteadily to his feet, gave a feeble snarl and slunk out of the bar, accompanied by loud guffaws from the customers. The barman watched him go through the door and then turned to Junipa.

"You're not from around here, are you?"

"No."

"So where are you from?"

"I'd rather not say."

"You didn't just come here for a fruit juice."

Junipa hesitated, uncertain for a few moments how best to proceed. She decided to keep it simple.

"No, I am looking for someone."

The barman pursed his lips.

"Our customers don't like being looked for, if you get what I mean. They prefer everyone keeps their noses out of everyone else's business."

"Yes, I quite understand, but I'm trying to contact a very old friend, Maggie Gulliver. Have you ever heard of her?"

The barman eyed her very suspiciously.

"Even if I had, why would she come here?"

Junipa realized that the situation had become delicate. The only thing to do was to be straightforward and hope that it worked.

"I believe that she was trying to contact a Captain Sloakum. I take it that you know of him?"

The barman nodded cautiously.

"Yes, we know Captain Sloakum."

Being straightforward seemed only to be taking her so far. Junipa wondered whether a little creative extrapolation might work better.

"I know that she and Captain Sloakum have had their differences in the past. She is a little hot-headed and I was afraid she might take things too far, so I was hoping to be able to restrain her."

The barman let out a laugh.

"Restrain Maggie? Take more than you to do that! Yeah, you're right. She did come here to find Sloakum, and she was all riled up. She was going to cut him down where he stood. But he's a wily old bird. He started sweet-talking her and before you know it, they were on their way from here like a pair of lovebirds. Never seen anything like it."

Junipa could not contain her astonishment.

"What? Maggie and Sloakum were sworn enemies!"

"That's as maybe," said the barman, "but when there's talk of gold, people can get very friendly."

"What do you mean, gold?"

"What do you think I mean? Gold, the yellow shiny stuff. Sloakum said he was doing a big job for that Lord High Jackass of the Orsonians. He was getting paid in gold and Maggie could have some if she went in with him."

Junipa found she had difficulty taking the news in.

"Are you saying that she has joined forces with Sloakum?"

"That's what I'm saying. Like lovebirds, they were."

***

"This is an even bigger mess than I thought."

Junipa stared glumly ahead, as Orestia gave her a dressing-down.

"I expect we shall have to intervene now. How, I'm not sure, but I think we may have a little time. I assume Sloakum and Gulliver don't yet know where de la Beche is."

Junipa swallowed hard.

"I'm not sure about that."

"What do you mean?"

Junipa swallowed again.

"Well, um, I told Maggie that de la Beche was going to Libertania."

"What! Why?"

"It just slipped out when I was briefing her. I didn't think it mattered. She was going after Sloakum, not de la Beche. It never occurred to me that she would join up with Sloakum. I don't think it occurred to you either," she added.

22

Jim was just clearing up after the grog session when he saw Splenditheran's face appear on the big screen and heard de la Beche.

"Commander Splenditheran, how nice to see you again. To what do I owe this pleasure?"

Jim saw that Splenditheran looked worried, even slightly agitated, very different from his usual expression.

"Captain de la Beche, I owe you an apology."

"You do, darling? Accepted, I'm sure. What for, exactly?"

"I have just come from the most disturbing interrogation of my Chief of Staff. You were quite right. There was a plot against me and he was the chief plotter. It was only discovered by chance, when one of the miscreants accidentally sent a message to one of my most loyal operatives, who of course informed me immediately. We have now rounded up the entire cabal and they have given us full details of their dastardly conspiracy. Our interrogation methods are most thorough."

"I'm sure they are, darling. Quite right, too."

"They will, of course, receive their due punishment."

De la Beche nodded in acknowledgement.

"Absolutely. Show them no mercy."

"We certainly will not, Captain. As you know, we are of the Non-Inflationary denomination of the Sacrosanctity of Reason. The punishment allowed by our creed for such crimes is dissolution into constituent atoms by a beam of protons. For the smaller fry we will be lenient and begin at the neck and work upwards. It will be quick. For the ringleader, we will begin at his feet and work slowly upwards. He will remain conscious and watch his body slowly disappear. Most appropriate, don't you think?"

"Absolutely. Make the punishment fit the crime – that's what I always say."

Splenditheran paused for a few seconds before continuing.

"I have further information to impart, Captain, some of which concerns you."

"I'm all ears, Commander. Do continue."

"It transpires that my Chief of Staff had agreed some sort of non-aggression pact with the High Admiral of the Orsonian Empire – or *Lord* High Admiral, as I believe he now styles himself. They proposed jointly to invade the Arcturan Empire and divide the greater part of it among themselves. Can you imagine the result? There would be uproar! It would upset the equilibrium of the entire Galaxy. Wars would break out everywhere. It must not be allowed to happen."

"Quite right. Somebody has to look after the Galaxy."

"It also transpires, Captain, that the Admiral is now aware of your role in the attempted retrieval of the Kwokkah and is, understandably I suppose, none too pleased about it. He has procured the service of a Captain Sloakum, a brigand, I believe, to deliver you to him."

Jim saw a wry smile appear on de la Beche's face.

"Ah yes, Sloakum. The Lord High Admiral always has such exquisite taste."

"I take it you are now at Planet Libertania. Does Sloakum know where you are?"

"Who knows, darling, who knows?"

23

Jim thought the saloon at *Dead Man's Chest* seemed quieter than before. He had returned with de la Beche, Doctor Culpepper, Bosun Bones, the Bold Deceiver and Major Schickelgrosser. De la Beche looked around at the company. "What to do next? At the moment we only have one clue to go on – Roy Pesshe, whoever or whatever he, she or it might be. *Galactopedia* is no help at all, as we have found, and that fount of all fantasies, the *Princ Ont*, even less so. Has anyone any suggestions?"

The longish silence was broken by Culpepper.

"Maybe it's simple. Roy Pesshe is just a person who knows something."

De la Beche shook his head.

"I'm surprised at you, Sawbones. Simplicity never appeals to me as an explanation. If somebody says something is simple, then either they are trying to pull the wool over my eyes, or they have no idea what they are talking about. Complexity beyond understanding is nearly always the reality."

Culpepper persisted.

"Perhaps so, but this is not the place to look for complicated answers. Perhaps if we just asked a few simple questions we might get some clues. Why don't we ask the barman? He seems to know what goes on around here."

De la Beche shrugged. "Why not?" He summoned the barman.

"Another round of your excellent potions for my friends, barman, if you please. There is one other thing you might be able to help us with. Do the words 'Roy Pesshe' mean anything to you?"

The barman shook his head.

"No. Never heard nothing like that."

De la Beche pulled out his wallet and began fingering it.

"Are you absolutely sure? Is there anyone that might know something?"

The barman eyed the wallet and thought for some moments.

"Tell the truth, I did hear something once. An old timer called Dick McGoon was in here, in his cups. He'd been given a hard time somewhere and kept muttering something that sounded like Roy Pesshe. Dunno what he meant by it, but he did know everybody once."

De la Beche nodded and pulled out a token from his wallet.

"Keep the change. Now, can you tell us where we might find this Mister McGoon?"

The barman laughed.

"You'll be lucky. He lives up in the hills all by himself. He don't go nowhere now, and he definitely don't like strangers."

As the barman spoke, Jim noticed that Bosun Bones had become excited.

"Dick McGoon, blow me down if it ain't that old bilge rat, Dick McGoon. There can't be two of 'em. We was shipmates on Sloakum's ship long ago. So here's where he ended up. I always wondered."

All eyes turned towards Bones.

"Don't keep us in suspense, darling," said de la Beche. "What do you mean 'ended up'?"

Bosun Bones chortled.

"Cap'n Sloakum was going to have him strung up for being ten sheets to the wind while he was coxswain. Only he jumped ship and, not only that, he took half Sloakum's treasure chest with him. Sloakum was livid. He was slittin' gizzards for ages after that."

"Most interesting. Did you ever hear him talk of a Roy Pesshe?" asked de la Beche.

"Never did, Cap'n, but then there's things sailors never talk of. They'd be taking a chance with Lady Luck, if you know what I mean."

"Did he ever sail with Captain Blacksabre?" enquired Doctor Culpepper.

"Maybe. What was his ship, Doc?"

"The *Faerie Queene.*"

"I think he did. I seem to remember him mentioning it. He'd sailed on a lot of ships before I ever clapped eyes on him. He was the best coxswain there was. He could handle any ship, even when he'd had more'n a few."

"The reason I asked," said Culpepper, "is that I once sailed with Blacksabre, and one of his crew told me that that when he was here on Libertania he and some others had found a way to get to Utrophia. They thought they would find easy pickings, but instead they were sent packing by a bunch of monks. Do you think Dick McGoon could have been one of them?"

Bosun Bones nodded vigorously.

"If there was pickings, easy or hard, Dick McGoon would be up for it, Doc. There wasn't nothing he wouldn't do to get his paws on loot."

"Perhaps Mister McGoon is worth talking to," said de la Beche. He turned to the barman, who had been listening to the conversation. "Exactly where might we find him?"

The barman shrugged and pointed out of the window towards a row of distant hills that stretched from horizon to horizon.

"How would I know? He's somewhere out there. I tell you who might know," he added. "Rosco. He goes to see him sometimes."

"You mean the fellow who has rats for friends?" asked Jim

The barman seemed surprised but then recognized Jim.

"Yeah. I remember now. You and this geezer," he pointed at Schickelgrosser, "had a little run in with him, didn't you? Don't take him with you. Rosco never forgets a face and he don't like what he did to his rats."

They left the Major in the bar. In the road outside they found Rosco giggling and snorting as two rats nibbled his buttocks. On seeing de la Beche, dressed as he was in a halterneck, zebra-print jumpsuit with wide, flared trousers, red patent-leather boots and jaunty, gold-trimmed cap, he sprang to his feet and saluted, uttering something that Jim could not catch.

"Rosco, darling," said de la Beche, "so good to see you – and your little friends here." He pointed to the rats, which had shrunk back, seemingly alarmed at his appearance. "So charming. They must be a great comfort to you."

Rosco grunted again.

"Now Rosco," continued de la Beche, "I have a little request of you. I understand another of your friends is a Mister Dick McGoon."

Another grunt, this time a little more animated.

"Well as it happens, by a remarkable coincidence, one of our number, my esteemed colleague Bosun Bones, is a very old friend of Mister McGoon and, as he is here, would very much like to renew the acquaintance. He would be very grateful if you could let him know where Mister McGoon lives, so that he can visit him."

Rosco grew a little agitated.

"Rosco no tell. Dick say no tell."

De la Beche smiled benevolently.

"Oh come now, Rosco. It may be Bosun Bones' last chance to see one of his oldest friends. You wouldn't want him not to have that chance, would you?"

Rosco's agitation increased.

"No, no. Rosco not tell. Dick say he kill Rosco if Rosco tell."

De la Beche nodded in seeming assent.

"Oh well, if that's the case, I suppose we must leave it there." He patted Rosco and then looked down at one of the rats. "Am I mistaken or do you think there may be something wrong with that animal, Doctor?"

Culpepper gave a puzzled look and then understood. He leaned down to examine it more closely. As he did so it appeared to slump to the floor and remained motionless.

"I fear you may be right, Captain. A case of *lymphodema rodentiae,* quite advanced. Invariably fatal in this type of animal, unless treated."

Rosco looked at the Doctor and then his face crumpled. He fell to the floor sobbing and began stroking the rat.

"No, no, Tilly not die. No."

De la Beche shook his head.

"Very sad, Doctor. Is there no hope?"

Culpepper continued his examination.

"Well, Captain, normally I would say no hope whatsoever, but it so happens that I do have the one medicine that I believe is effective against this most virulent malady." He hesitated. "However ..."

"However what, Doctor?" asked de la Beche.

"However, Captain, I only have a very small dosage and it must be reserved for emergencies on board ship."

De la Beche smiled sadly.

"There you are, Rosco darling. Nothing to be done, I'm afraid. I think we should ask the good Doctor to put this poor animal out of its misery."

Rosco's sobs increased in intensity.

"No, no. Rosco love Tilly. Tilly not die. Please, please, you save her."

Culpepper and de la Beche looked at each other, then de la Beche turned back to Rosco.

"Well, darling, I must say we are most touched by your devotion to poor Tilly. It does you great credit, but, if we were to agree to part with some of our very valuable medicine, we would need something in return."

Rosco's expression lightened and he gave a little grunt of acknowledgement. De la Beche continued.

"We would like you to take us to meet your friend, Mister Dick McGoon."

Rosco's expression darkened again momentarily and then became one of desperation. He looked down at Tilly, then up at de la Beche and the Doctor, then down again.

"OK, OK. You save Tilly and Rosco take you see Dick."

"De la Beche smiled benignly and put an arm round Rosco's shoulders.

"Now then, Rosco, dry your eyes. I'm sure Tilly will be fine, won't she Doctor?"

Culpepper nodded and waved an implement over Tilly.

"This dose now and the second when we get back. She'll be as right as rain after that."

Tilly rose quickly and showed no reaction beyond a slight twitch of the nose.

"There, she didn't feel a thing," said de la Beche. "Now Rosco, darling, lead us to Mister McGoon."

24

They tramped across miles of flat, sandy scrubland. In the enervating heat, Jim was continually fending off the large, biting flies, as were all his companions except de la Beche, who had unrolled a veil from his turban that covered his face and neck and rolled down over his shoulders.

"A little thing I invented for the tropics, darling," he said, as Jim stared in envy. "Amazing how useful it can be sometimes. I have a particular abhorrence of mastication by creepy-crawlies. So undignified."

Eventually they came to the foothills of what appeared in the distance to be a large mountain range. As they rose, the heat lessened a little and the flies became smaller, but even more numerous and savage. The vegetation increased until eventually the path along which Rosco was leading them was just wide enough for single file. The rough, thorny scrub and bushes tore at their clothes and the flies buzzed almost continuously about their ears. Every so often Jim heard squeaks and grunts from something near them.

"Rats," said Rosco, as Jim looked alarmed at one particularly piercing squeal. "Rats my friends. If Rosco no here, they bite you, bad."

Eventually, after several hours more, they came to a clearing. In the middle Jim saw what appeared to be a small, ramshackle wooden house, surrounded by an equally ramshackle picket fence. Rosco stopped and pointed.

"Dick live there."

"Splendid," said de la Beche. "I was beginning to think we would never get there. Lead on Rosco, and introduce us to your friend."

Rosco shrank back.

"Rosco no go. You go."

Just then there was aloud bang and something whipped through the bushes beside them. They heard a loud, gruff voice.

"One step further and I'll blast ye all to smithereens! Get back to where ye came from. Ye've no business here!"

They dived for cover behind the nearest bush, crouching down further as another fusillade tore through the leaves above them.

"What in heavens is that weapon?" asked de la Beche of Bosun Bones. "Whoever heard of a bang like that? Effective, nevertheless. Is your friend Mister McGoon always this welcoming?"

"He was always a bit cantankerous, Cap'n, if you know what I mean. He don't take to people that easy."

"I think we can see that," said de la Beche. "Now Bosun, since he is an old acquaintance of yours, perhaps you could try to persuade him that we mean him no harm."

Bones looked very doubtful.

"Talking never persuaded him of anything, Cap'n. He was never one for conversation."

"Well do try, darling. Remind him of your old times together. Perhaps that will lighten his mood."

Bones looked even more doubtful, but cupped his hands to his mouth and shouted out.

"Hello, Dick. It's Bosun Ben Bones here. Remember me? We was shipmates together with Cap'n Sloakum. I heard you was in these parts, so I thought to meself I must look up me old shipmate, Dick. We'll have a good chinwag about the times we had together. Great old times, weren't they, Dick?"

Another shot rang out. Jim felt something pass perilously close to his cheek.

"Ye always were a no-good, snivelling, bilge rat, Benjamin Bones, and by the sound of ye, things haven't changed. Why Sloakum never had ye dancing the yardarm jig I'll never know.

He must have gone soft in his old age. Don't give me any of your good old times. I said to meself on the day I jumped that pox ridden ship that, if I never saw Sloakum or any of his scurvy crew again, it would be too soon."

This time, two shots rang out. Jim looked around in alarm but none of them seemed to be hit. The sound of the shots seemed to revive Schickelgrosser, who up till then had marched morosely and mostly silently along.

"I say we take the varmint, Captain. Give me five minutes with him and he'll be singing like an Astromican bluebird."

"I take your point, Major," said de la Beche. "Nostalgia doesn't seem to have done the trick. I think we will have to try a different tack. Let's retreat a little." They went back further into the bushes. De la Beche turned to Rosco."

"Is Mister McGoon alone in there?"

Rosco nodded.

"Dick all alone, only his cat. He no like anyone only Rosco, and now he no like Rosco, because I bring you."

"Oh don't fret, darling. I'm sure he'll get over it once we have a chance to explain to him why we have come. To do that we may, as the Major says, have to get a little bit closer to the irascible Mister McGoon and that, I think, will need weapons. I have my personal blaster, of course, but it may be a little too lethal for the occasion. We do need Mister McGoon to be alive to tell us what we need to know. Does anyone else have something that might be useful?"

Jim, Culpepper and Bosun Bones shook their heads. Schickelgrosser looked down shamefacedly at his shoes. The Bold Deceiver drew his sword and swished it extravagantly in the air. De la Beche looked on approvingly.

"Exactly what we need. Cold steel, always very persuasive – and with style. Now we need a plan. Major, as a military man, perhaps you could suggest a course of action."

Schickelgrosser looked momentarily surprised, then gratified.

"Well, Captain, first we need to know the territory. Is there another door to that building?"

They turned to Rosco.

"No other door. Only one."

Schickelgrosser nodded.

"Right. We need a distraction, if we're going to get in. Here's the plan. Two of us will go round the back and make a noise, so he thinks we want to get in through a window. We'll keep him tied down, while the rest of you get in the front door and take him."

De la Beche beamed.

"Splendid, Major. Simple, elegant and sound. I think we all agree." The others all nodded their approval. "I suggest you take Bosun Bones with you to the back. Bosun, you engage Mister McGoon in conversation again. Give as good as you get with the insults, this time. That will keep him occupied. You, Major, will then fire a single shot with my blaster. Make sure you don't hit anything. I have set the acoustics on, so it has a very distinctive sound. That will be our signal to go in through the front door and allow the Bold Deceiver's sabre to open the discussion."

Schickelgrosser drew himself up to attention.

"Ready to go when you give the word, Captain."

"Off you both go, then."

There was no obvious path. Schickelgrosser and Bones started to push their way through the thick scrub. They had only gone a short way when Schickelgrosser felt a sharp pain in his ankle. He looked down and thought he saw a brown shape disappearing into the bush. Then Bones let out a yell.

"Something bit my leg!"

Schickelgrosser grabbed his arm and said, in an angry whisper: "Quiet! You'll let him know we're here. Wait till we get round the back."

"It hurts."

Schickelgrosser had little sympathy.

"It's a little scratch, just a rat bite. You'll live, sailor. Keep going."

Almost immediately Schickelgrosser felt another bite, then another, and Bones too started agitatedly kicking at whatever was biting him. Under attack, Schickelgrosser's military training kicked in. Almost unthinkingly, he drew his weapon and fired. The biting stopped and he saw several brown shapes scurry away into the bushes.

The sound of Schickelgrosser's shot reached the others.

"That's my blaster," said de la Beche, "but it's too soon. They can't have made it to the back yet. Better hold back."

Too late. The Bold Deceiver had drawn his sword and, with a mighty yell, dashed forward, vaulted over the fence and was running towards the door. A shot rang out and Jim saw the Bold Deceiver lurch back and then fall to the floor. For a moment, Jim thought that he must be dead, but then he saw the Deceiver start crawling back towards the fence, stagger to his feet and fall over the fence as another shot whistled after him. Jim watched as he crawled along the bottom of the fence, until he was out of McGoon's sight, before getting to his feet and limping back towards them.

"Let that be a lesson to you, darling," said de la Beche, as the Bold Deceiver attempted to staunch the blood from his wounded leg. "Impetuosity is never an appealing trait, even in one as young as you. Doctor," he said turning to Culpepper, "doubtless there is something you can do."

Culpepper knelt down to examine the wound. He waved an instrument over it.

"Very odd. It appears to have been some sort of ballistic weapon. There are pellets lodged in the flesh." He gazed at the instrument dial. "They appear to be lead. Never seen anything like it. I shall have to extract them by hand."

He took a pair of tweezers from his bag and began plucking out the pellets, to the accompaniment of anguished groans from the Bold Deceiver.

"That's the last of them. The wound is only superficial. This should put it right."

He took another implement and ran it over the wound, applying what seemed to be a skin that covered the bleeding flesh.

"Feeling better now, darling?" asked de la Beche.

The Bold Deceiver rose to his feet and Jim could see from his face that the pain had gone. He picked up his sword, which had been laying on the ground and brandished it in the direction of McGoon's house.

"The slayer of the one hundred monstrous Snellnooks of the Halls of Croesovia, is never vanquished in combat. Onwards!"

"Not so fast," said de la Beche. "We need to rethink our strategy."

As he spoke, Schickelgrosser and Bosun Bones appeared from out of the bushes. Bones was limping, while Schickelgrosser looked distinctly sheepish.

"Pesky rats! Damn near everywhere. You can't see 'em and you can't keep 'em off. Only thing I could do was shoot at 'em and I don't think I hit a darned one. I guess McGoon must have heard, eh?"

De la Beche and Culpepper exchanged glances.

"I'm afraid he did and the Bold Deceiver thought your shot was the signal for him to cut his customary dash. Unfortunately he was on the receiving end of whatever Mister McGoon is firing. So now we need a little rethink about what we do next."

Schickelgrosser grimaced. "I tell you this as a soldier Captain, you won't get through those bushes without a weapon. Damn rats will eat you alive."

They pondered on this for several moments before Rosco spoke.

"You go with Rosco. Rats no bite you then."

The rest of the company turned towards Rosco with varying degrees of incomprehension.

"What do you mean?" said de la Beche. "Why would the rats leave you alone?"

"Rats my friends," said Rosco. "They no bite me. If you with me, you my friends too. They no bite you."

All the company looked sceptical, except Jim.

"He may be right. We weren't attacked by the rats when we came here and Rosco was with us."

"Good point, Jim" said de la Beche. "In the absence of any better idea, it's worth a try. Are you both willing?"

Schickelgrosser nodded; Bones seemed less enthusiastic. Rosco stared at them

"Rosco no go if you hurt rats. No hurt Dick, too. Dick my friend."

"Any friend of yours is a friend of ours, darling," said de la Beche. "Rest assured. We won't harm a hair of Mister McGoon's head. We just want a little word with him."

Rosco nodded. "Come with Rosco." and walked towards the bushes. Schickelgrosser and Bones followed, making sure they kept close. Several minutes passed before they heard the sound of breaking glass and then the Bosun's voice.

"You still in there, Dick McGoon? What way was that to greet an old shipmate?"

McGoon's voice boomed back.

"Don't come the old shipmate with me, you spawn of a threepenny upright, Benjamin Bones. Be off with you and your gab or I'll come out and tan your hide with lead."

Bones yelled back, several notches louder.

"Three sheets to the wind Dick, as you always was. You couldn't hit an Orian hippogryph if your head was stuck up its backside."

McGoon's yells became louder and almost incoherent. Then they heard the boom of the blaster. De la Beche put a restraining arm on the Bold Deceiver.

"Now remember, stealth is our watchword. He mustn't hear us coming."

The Deceiver drew his sword and they climbed over the fence and moved silently towards the door. De la Beche put his finger to his lips and then very gently tried the latch. It gave and he opened the door very slowly. There was a slight squeak from the hinges, but this was drowned out by the furious altercation between Bones and McGoon, which had reached a new pitch in intensity. Oaths from the pirate lexicon were being tossed about with abandon. They found themselves in a room furnished only with a couple of rickety chairs. On the opposite wall was a door slightly ajar, through which they could hear McGoon. De la Beche tiptoed over to the door, peered through the opening, and motioned to the Deceiver. He pointed to the door and the Deceiver swept through, sword first.

"Have at you, Sirrah! One move, and you go to meet your ancestors."

De la Beche swung the door open and Jim saw McGoon, weapon in hand, framed in a window with the Bold Deceiver's sword poised between his shoulders. For a second his yells stopped, then, with a furious oath, he attempted to turn round. In a blur, Jim saw the weapon sail across the room and McGoon was upended on his back, with the Bold Deceiver's sword pointing at his throat.

"Prepare to suffer the fate of the evil Drogon of Arithmethetea!" announced the Deceiver, as his sword stroked McGoon's windpipe.

"Not a fate to be envied, darling," interjected de la Beche, as he gazed down at McGoon. "One that you could easily avoid if you could manage a little chat. We merely seek information."

McGoon uttered incoherent growls and whimpers. De la Beche gestured to the Deceiver to lift his sword and allow McGoon to get to his feet. He yelled to Schickelgrosser and Bosun Bones that they could now come into the house.

"Now, Mister McGoon," said de la Beche, "allow me to introduce myself. I am Sir Sechaverell de la Beche, Captain of HMS *Bountiful,* the renowned privateer. You may have heard of me and, if not, I can only pity your ignorance. We just want a little chat with you."

McGoon's gaze flicked disbelievingly between de la Beche and the Deceiver.

"What about?"

"Do the words Roy Pesshe mean anything to you?"

A startled look flashed momentarily across McGoon's face, before it resumed its sullen expression.

"Never heard of him."

De la Beche shook his head and smiled.

"Who said anything about it being a him – or a her or an it, for that matter? Please don't try and pull the wool over our eyes, darling. You clearly know something. The Bold Deceiver here is the despatcher of countless monstrous Snellnooks and would have no qualms in despatching you too. Do tell us all you know about this Roy Pesshe."

The Deceiver lifted his sword. McGoon looked at each of the party in turn and then shrugged.

"Do yer worst. Kill me and ye'll never know. Don't kill me and I'll never tell."

For several seconds there was silence. Then Bosun Bones spoke up.

"I think I know how to make him talk, Cap'n." He tapped the psittacoid on the beak. "Let's see what ye've got to say to Doris, Dick."

Doris began to utter a stream of what seemed to Jim to be high-pitched squeaks. The effect on McGoon was almost immediate. An expression, first of astonishment, then of terror, spread across his face. He fell to his knees, sobbing, and begged for it to stop. Doris squeaked remorselessly on as McGoon lay writhing on the floor, tears streaming down his face.

De la Beche eyed the helpless McGoon.

"Remarkable, darling. How did Doris manage that?"

"It all goes back, Cap'n, to when Dick was marooned on a planet where they had their own funny lingo and they believed in ghosts. Dick told me once that the ghosts would come to him when he was sleeping and swear at him, telling him that they would do all sorts of horrible things to him, things that he could never imagine could be done. Scared out of his wits, he was. He was still trembling, years after, when he told me about it. Us sailors are like that, Cap'n. We're all afeard of ghosts. Now Doris knows that lingo, so she's pswearing at him in it and it's brought it all back. Looking at him, I think he's about ready to talk."

Bosun Bones tapped Doris on the beak again, and the squeaking stopped. Jim watched as McGoon's expressions ran the gamut from relief to resignation.

"Alright, ye win. I have heard of Roy Pesshe, but ye'll never find him."

"Why wouldn't we find him? Where's he hiding?" said de la Beche.

McGoon grunted.

"He ain't hiding. He's somewhere where ye can't go. Ye ever heard of Utrophia?"

"We certainly have, darling. What do you know about it?"

McGoon's expression darkened.

"Went there once. Never again."

"Well if you went there, why can't we?"

McGoon gave a half smile.

"Because ye don't know how to get there."

"You're going to tell us how, darling, otherwise I shall hand you over to the tender mercies of the Bold Deceiver."

"Do what ye like and damn yer eyes. I can't tell ye, because I don't know meself."

De la Beche looked puzzled.

"You managed to get there, but you don't know how?"

McGoon nodded.

"In a way. I'll tell ye the story. Long time ago, when I told Sloakum to sling his hook, I took a nice little haul with me, as Benjamin Bones probably told ye. So I bought this little ship, lovely little rig she was, called the *Molly Malone*. We had a fine old time. Took a ton of prizes and one of them was carrying the Grand Panjellycum, or whatever he was called, of some planet I'd never heard of. He was very full of himself and his God, calling down all sorts of curses from his God on us. What we wasn't going to suffer in the hereafter couldn't be suffered, if ye see what I mean. Pretty soon we'd heard enough, so we stuck a stick of bang-bang up his backside and put him overboard. When it went off, there was bits of him over half the Galaxy. How we roared. Even his God would have had a hard time putting him back together for his eternal reward.

"It was a pretty poor prize. Nothing worth much. When we got back on our ship, my First Mate, Jason, found a little glass ball in one of the boxes that we took. If you rubbed it it lit up and all sorts of funny signs floated across it. I thought it was just a plaything, but Jason was a bit of a brainbox and he reckoned that all them signs must be some sort of secret message. He said we have to come here and talk to the Coders. Have ye heard of the Coders?"

"We have come across them, darling. Rather an unusual bunch."

"That's as maybe, but Jason reckoned that they were the only ones that could make sense of it. So he took it to them and when he came back, he said he was right. Them signs were a puzzle, and the Coders had solved it for him. It turned out to be the way to get to somewhere called Utrophia. We'd never heard of it, but, when we found out that there was just a load of god-botherers there, we reckoned that there would be plenty of easy pickings, so we had to go."

"I understand the pickings weren't quite as easy as you imagined," said de la Beche.

McGoon grimaced.

"When we were in orbit, our detectors said there was any amount of gold and silver and everything else there. Ye wouldn't believe how much. We landed where we reckoned there was the most gold and as soon as we did we were surrounded by hundreds of whirling madmen, shouting and screaming and throwing things at the lander. So we thought we would give them a taste of our blasters, but they didn't work. They threw themselves at us. We hit them with everything we could lay our hands on, but still they kept coming, and in the end we couldn't stop them. We lost a couple of the crew. Torn to pieces, they were, before I could get the hatches shut and take off, with half a dozen of the madmen still hanging on."

"A salutary lesson," said de la Beche, "but where does Roy Pesshe come into all this."

"When Jason bought the ball back from the Coders he rubbed it and letters appeared on it saying 'Seek ye Roy Pesshe.' Then he said it sent the instructions for our guidance system to get to Utrophia. After that, it just showed nothing. I didn't know what it all meant. Jason handled all that stuff. It was gobbledygook to me."

"Where is the ball now?" asked de la Beche.

McGoon shrugged.

"Maybe on the *Molly Malone* – somewhere."

"What do you mean, 'somewhere'?"

"I haven't got her any more. Lost her in a card game. The devil takes me sometimes. I'd lost a packet, so I had to go all in to get it back, but Lady Luck had it in for me that day. I lost the lot and now I'm marooned here."

There was silence for a while, as the company digested this news. Then de la Beche spoke.

"I'm not sure Mister McGoon has told us everything. I rather suspect he knows exactly where this ball is. Perhaps Bosun you could allow Doris to ask him."

The look of terror returned to McGoon's face.

"Damn yer eyes! It's in one of the boxes in the back room there. It's some of my old stuff that I never bothered to throw away, but it ain't going to be much use to ye, lest ye can work out what it says."

They set to examining the contents of the crowded room. Most of the things were ill-gotten relics of raids McGoon and his crew had made in their glory days – tatty knick-knacks and artefacts of little value, not even worth losing in a card game. Eventually, at the bottom of one box, Jim spied a small globe. He picked it up gingerly. It was white, lightly-mottled with blue, and surprisingly heavy. He handed it to de la Beche, who ran his fingers over it. No signs of any sort appeared. De la Beche handed it to Mister Betelgeuse, who turned it over and examined it carefully with an implement he took out from one of his pockets.

"It is definitely some sort of device, Captain. However, I think that whatever energy source powered it has been exhausted. It is not clear how it might be replenished."

De la Beche turned to McGoon.

"Is this what we were looking for?"

"That's it," said McGoon, "and much good may it do ye."

De la Beche took the ball from Mr Betelgeuse and rolled it around his hand.

"I think we will take this back to the *Bountiful*. We must have something there that can unlock its little secrets."

25

The Lord High Admiral of the Orsonian Battle Fleet stared glumly at the miserable specimen of bureaucratic life that was Civil Servant 21436. Even the thought of his four wives, sixteen mistresses and numerous progeny failed to lift the gloom. To the contrary, thoughts of wives and mistresses only reminded him of the cacophony of complaint when he had first tried to relieve them of their precious gold jewellery. Now it was going to start all over again. He fixed Civil Servant 21436 with his most baleful stare, the one intended to induce bowel-loosening fear in all who experienced it.

"Tell me exactly what happened."

Far from being frightened, Civil Servant 21436 was exultant at the turn of events and had to struggle mightily to display the expression of submissive concern that the Admiral expected.

"I'm not sure we know *exactly* what happened, Lord High Admiral. We're still piecing things together. What *seems* to have happened is that Splenditheran found out about the plot against him and rounded up the plotters. They all suffered the usual fate."

The Admiral digested this news.

"Do they have any suspicions that, ah, others might have been involved?"

Civil Servant 21436's exultation rose a notch or two.

"I'm afraid that they do."

The Admiral's eyes narrowed.

"What makes you think that?"

"They seem to suspect us. Their Battle Fleet has been placed on raised alert and freight and insurance rates have rocketed. It's impossible to import anything from outside the Empire."

"Nothing can be imported?"

"Absolutely nothing."

The Admiral's alarm mounted and his eyes narrowed further as he scrutinized the civil servant's expression, wondering if he knew why exactly he was asking that question. Civil Servant 21436 looked back at the Admiral wondering whether the Admiral knew that he knew exactly why he was asking that question. Since the de la Beche debacle, the Admiral had secretly secured deliveries of limited supplies of Chelodoney, using a complicated route involving several parties, all of which charged extortionate rates for their services. These were reserved for the Orsonian elite, all of whom were sworn to secrecy. Civil Servant 21436 was not among them, but had found out because of the Admiral's incompetence in using supposedly secure communication channels.

The Admiral decided that it was time to exercise his preeminent talent – blame diversion.

"Do you think they found out about the agreement that you concocted with their Chief of Staff?"

Civil Servant 21436 blinked, all exultation vanished.

"I beg your pardon, Lord High Admiral. Do you mean the pact that you instructed me to draw up between the Orsonian Empire and the Southern Cross Federation?"

The Admiral waved his hand airily.

"I don't remember *instructing* you, Civil Servant 21436. I merely said this was an interesting proposal from this so-called Chief of Staff, who turns out to have been an impostor and a traitor, and asked you to follow up with some details. It seems you may have gone further than you should."

Civil Servant 21436 had to think hard and fast. He was in trouble, but he thought he had one last trump card.

"I believe I was following your instructions on the pact with the Southern Cross Federation, Lord High Admiral, just as I believed I was following them concerning Captain Sloakum."

The Admiral felt a twinge of anxiety. He had put the Sloakum business out of his mind, assuming that Civil Servant 21436 had managed to fob him off, at whatever cost, and all mention of gold had disappeared. Now, he had just a scintilla of doubt.

"Yes, of course, the question of Sloakum is an entirely different matter. I take it that it has all been dealt with?"

Civil Servant 21436 decided that he had to push home his advantage.

"Not quite, Lord High Admiral. I have only managed to contact Captain Sloakum once to inform him that we wished to amend certain aspects of our agreement. I received a very abusive message in return, the gist of which was that he had no intention of amending anything and – I paraphrase here – it would be rather the worse for you if you persisted. Of course, I did not trouble you with this information because I assumed that this was simply an opening gambit and that we would sort things out in the negotiations, but so far I have been unable to contact him again. He seems to have cut off all communication."

The Admiral added exasperation to his anxiety.

"Are you utterly incompetent, Civil Servant 21436? There must be some way of reaching him? Where do we know he was last?"

"We understand that he went to Baccanorgia, the capital city of Arctura."

The Admiral's temper rose.

"What are you waiting for? Go there, find him and don't come back until you have sorted everything out."

Civil Servant 21436 closed the trap.

"I'm afraid that may not be possible, Lord High Admiral. We have been trying to communicate with Arctura but you know how chaotic they are. All we got back were garbled messages or snatches of songs. Now we have just received news that the Southern Cross Federation have told the Arcturans about the supposed plot and the Arcturans have cut all communications between us."

Things looked bad. Could they get worse?

"What about de la Beche? Do we know where he is?"

"I'm afraid not, Lord High Admiral. He seems to have disappeared completely."

"Is he still after the Kwokkah?"

"As Commander Splenditheran is still leader of the Southern Cross Federation, we must assume so."

"And the Nullarboreans? What are they doing?"

"Still a great deal of religious ferment there, Lord High Admiral. The region is becoming very unstable."

Things had got worse, very much worse.

"Let me sum this up, Civil Servant 21436. We have no idea where either Sloakum or de la Beche are, the Arcturans are against us, the Southern Cross are against us and the Nullarboreans are teetering. Is that all the bad news you have to tell me or have you some more?"

Civil Servant 21436 hesitated.

"Well ..."

The Admiral's eyes widened.

"Well what?"

"We're not quite sure. About the time when de la Beche, ahem, about then, our signals unit picked up some unusual chatter. It just looked like noise, so they didn't think it was significant, but now they think maybe it was."

"What do they mean, 'maybe'?"

"Well it now appears to be some sort of communication between de la Beche's ship and ..."

"Spit it out, Civil Servant 21436. Who?"

Civil Servant 21436 realized there was nothing else for it.

"The Feminarchs."

The bellow almost blew him off his feet. The Admiral, crimson faced, rose and swept past him out of the office and away, doubtless to assuage his anger among his wives and mistresses. Civil Servant 21436, no wife and no mistress, stood and contemplated the futility of his existence.

26

The strings hanging from her hat swished from side to side as Maggie Gulliver flicked her head in an effort to keep off the flies that continuously assaulted her face. Sweat dripped off the end of her nose. They were walking along a path that wound its way through an arid landscape, thinly populated with short scrubby thorn bushes. She glanced to her left to see flies veer sharply away as they came close to Sloakum.

"It's too hot, Jonah Sloakum. I can't stand this heat, nor these damn flies. Why did ye make me come here?"

"Because here's where ye said he would be," snarled Sloakum.

Maggie threw up her arms in exasperation, scattering a swarm of flies.

"I didn't mean come down here. He wouldn't have come down here neither. It would have messed with his fancy frocks. We could have waited for him up there and blasted him to pieces when he showed his face."

Sloakum grunted dismissively.

"He's too fly to let us do that to him, besides the deal is we deliver him to His High and Mightyness, all trussed up in one piece. That's the way we get our gold. He'll have been here all right. We need to find out what he's been up to."

They walked up a low hill. At the top Maggie viewed in the distance a motley collection of buildings.

"Davy Jones," said Sloakum. "Long time since I was here, but, if he's been anywhere, it'll be here."

They walked down the hill and at the outskirts of the town they came across a large billboard.

Rat Baiting

Today at the Yo Ho Ho Arena

Rats! Rats! Rats!

The biggest baddest rats you have ever seen!

No quarter given

Best odds guaranteed

Sloakum scanned the billboard with evident appreciation.

"Rat-baitin', Maggie. I think we'll have ourselves some of that."

"I thought we had come to this hellhole to find Fancypants, not to watch some damn rats," shouted Maggie exasperated.

"We'll find him, don't ye worry," said Sloakum, "but no harm in a little fun before we do."

They made their way into the town and followed a sign to the stadium. As they arrived, they joined a stream of others through the gate.

"The fun's just startin'," said Sloakum, seemingly in a better mood than Maggie had ever seen him before.

They sat down and watched the preliminaries. A brass band marched round the arena, playing hopelessly off-tune, to the jeers of the spectators, some of whom threw food and other missiles at them. Then a fanfare blasted out over the public address system, followed by an equally loud voice.

"Ladies and gentlemen, welcome to the rat-baiting capital of the Galaxy. This afternoon we have, for your delectation and appreciation, six sizzling contests. We have the best and bravest rat fighters taking on our pack of the biggest and baddest rats you can find anywhere. Which will win and which will lose? That's for you to decide. You can bet on winners and losers, you can bet on how long they last, you can bet on who loses a limb. You can make your own bet on anything you fancy and we guarantee to give you the best odds. Get over to the Tote windows now and place your bets – and who knows, make your fortune."

Sloakum's mood brightened a little further with the announcement.

"I'm goin' to have me a few bets, Maggie. Are ye coming with me?"

Maggie shook her head.

"I ain't one for bettin', Jonah Sloakum. I've lost too many, most of 'em to the likes of ye."

"Have it yer own way," said Sloakum and headed for the Tote.

The cashier looked suspiciously at Sloakum as he appeared in the window. Even by the less than dapper standards of their usual clientele, Sloakum, with his wart-ridden face, straggly beard and eyepatch, was repulsive.

"Can I help you?"

"I don't want yer help. I want to bet."

The cashier stiffened.

"No need to be like that. What do you want to bet on?"

Sloakum looked at the odds on the booth wall.

"What will ye give me for rats to win in five minutes in the first three?"

The cashier consulted his terminal.

"Four to one in the first, five to one in the second and thirteen to two in the third."

Sloakum spat. "Ye're a bunch of poxy swindlers. What about an accumulator?"

"Just multiply the odds," said the cashier, oblivious to the insult. "That would be," he consulted his terminal again, "a hundred and thirty to one."

Slaokum spat again and slapped a token down.

"Ye take Galactos?"

"Of course."

"Then give me a split on the lot."

The cashier nodded and printed out the ticket. Sloakum returned to his seat to find Maggie chewing on a large roll she had bought from one of the vendors walking round. He took out a large fob watch from his top pocket.

"Let's see what these fleabags are made of, Maggie."

The fanfare sounded again and the kennel was wheeled to the middle of the arena. A gate opened and, to the roar of the crowd, out ran half a dozen rats. They ran round the arena several times before one approached the open door of the kennel. It poked its head in. only to withdraw it with a yelp as the crowd laughed. Another rat tried its luck with the same result. Then suddenly two rats jumped in at the same time, almost disappearing. They began shaking their bodies violently and slowly backing out of the kennel, the crowd roaring them on. As they emerged, the spectators could see that they each had their jaws clamped on the leg of what looked like a young female. The other rats quickly joined in, seizing parts of her body and she was dragged screaming into the middle of the arena. The crowd noise reached a crescendo; many were standing up waving their betting slips. A figure with a whip strode into the arena and began beating the rats until they let go and made for the exit to their cage.

"What's the verdict?" boomed the address system.

Boos went up from the spectators and many showed a thumbs down. The address system sounded again.

"Take it away."

A gurney with two attendants appeared. They threw the still writhing and moaning female on and quickly wheeled it out. Sloakum had been examining his watch and muttered to himself.

"Three minutes, thirty-two."

The second bout went in much the same way, except that the 'fighter' was male, old, fat and had a long beard that one rat almost chewed off as it dragged him out. Sloakum looked at his watch again. "Four minutes, ten." The preparations were being made for the third bout. "If we win this 'un, Maggie, we're in the money."

Maggie snorted.

"Who's we, Jonah Sloakum? Ain't never seen ye give anything of your'n away."

Sloakum seemed affronted.

"I've promised ye gold, haven't I?"

"Only because I was going to blow yer head off."

Sloakum grunted and turned to watch. After their circuit, several rats tried to poke their heads into the kennel, only to be sharply rebuffed to the amusement of the crowd. Then one rat put its head in further and suddenly disappeared, as if pulled in. The crowd became excited, as loud yelps and screams were heard from the kennel. Then the rat was ejectedbodily from the kennel. It landed several metres away and lay prone. Two more rats dived in and exited almost immediately, squealing loudly. The spectators were in ecstasy as a hooded figure emerged from the kennel holding two large knives aloft and took their salute. Over their roars could be heard:

"We give you the great Androck. Undisputed king of the ratters. Take your trophy, Androck."

Androck lifted the tail of the prone rat and with a swift slash cut it off and held it up to the crowd, who roared more. So he cut its ears off. Then with a bow he marched off.

Sloakum was out of his seat, spitting with fury.

"The lyin', cheatin', scurvy scumbags. They put a ringer in to do me out of the winnins. I'll slit a few gizzards for this."

As he put his hand on his cutlass, Maggie drew her pistol from her pocket.

"Ye'll do no such thing, Jonah Sloakum. Try slittin' anything and ye'll get a taste of lead. We're here to find Fancypants, nothin' else."

Sloakum spluttered and swore as he looked hard at the pistol and then took his hand off his cutlass.

"Maybe I'll keep gizzard-slittin' for later Maggie, but I'll say this. I've taken a fancy to them rats. I fancy takin' a few back to the ship with me. A bit of rat-baitin' would keep the crew on their toes."

Maggie nodded.

"That sounds a good idea to me, Jonah Sloakum. Where do you think you might get 'em?"

***

The Ratmeister looked up with a start as Sloakum and Maggie swept into his cabin. He was about to yell for assistance when Sloakum spoke.

"Are ye in charge of the rats?"

The Ratmeister hesitated, unsure of how to answer.

"Why do you want to know?"

"I want to buy some."

The Ratmeister was completely bemused. He struggled to reply.

"Sorry, my hearing must be bad today I thought you said you wanted to buy rats."

"Nothin' wrong with yer hearin'. That's what I said."

The Ratmeister's bemusement only deepened.

"Why do you want them?"

Sloakum tried hard to keep his customary irritation in check.

"Never mind why. How much do ye want for 'em?"

The Ratmeister shook his head.

"Something funny is going on. Only the other day I had someone wanting to pay me for one of my fighters and now you want to buy rats. He was a bit different looking too," he added, eyeing Sloakum. "All dressed up in finery, a bit fancy, if you know what I mean."

Maggie reacted first.

"What was he like? Did he talk a bit lah-di-dah?"

"He did, come to think of it. Called me 'darling'. I haven't been called that in a long while."

Sloakum and Maggie exchanged glances.

"Where did he go from here?" asked Sloakum.

The Ratmeister shrugged.

"Don't remember. You could try asking in the *Dead Man's Chest*. That's the big tavern up the other end of town. Somebody there might knows what's going on. Now, about my rats. They don't come cheap. Have you any idea what it costs to train a rat?"

27

"Do we even know where Libertania is?"

Junipa's anxiety was rapidly mounting as she realized that she was being set up with yet another less-than-attractive assignment. Orestia remained unmoved.

"I have set our best cartographers on it. They believe they have located it."

"Yes, but what would I do if I go there? It could be very dangerous. I would need an armed guard."

Orestia demurred.

"I don't think so. You would only draw attention to yourself. From what I hear, the inhabitants are mostly harmless, mainly retired villains and cutthroats. Best to go alone. You are quite capable of looking after yourself."

Junipa could hardly disagree. Like most Feminarchs she had trained in martial arts since childhood and could also handle most personal protection weapons, but she would have preferred some company.

"Well, at least I must be able to call for support, if I feel threatened."

Orestia agreed. Junipa felt that she had no option but to go.

"What exactly is my mission?"

"Keep a very low profile, find out if de la Beche and Sloakum – and Maggie – are there, and what they are doing."

Junipa's anxiety was not assuaged.

"Is there any information we have about the place? Do we have any supporters there?"

Orestia consulted her communicator.

"There appears to be only one, although she is a judge."

Junipa's spirits lifted a little.

"That sounds promising. Do we know anything about her?"

"Only her name I'm afraid – Malignia Maleficia." She paused. "Rather unusual name. Still, it's all we have at the moment. I suggest you start with her and take it from there."

***

Junipa stared down at the desolate features of Libertania. She asked the ship's captain if they had detected anything else in orbit.

"Can't see anything, although that's not surprising. If they are here, they will probably be in stealth mode like us."

There was nothing else for it. She would have to go down.

"Where do you suggest I land?"

The captain surveyed a map of the surface on her screen.

"The only place of any real size is called Davy Jones."

Junipa gave a snort.

"Named after a male. That's all I need."

The captain gave a wry smile.

"These things are sent to try us. There's a spot just outside the town that looks suitable. You should be able to land unobserved. You will have to walk in though," she added. "It's a bit of a trek in the heat."

Junipa nodded glumly and asked her to organize the cutter for the descent.

***

Junipa walked along the same dirt track that Jim and Schickelgrosser had travelled, wilting as the heat, the humidity and the flies took their toll. As she came to the outskirts of the town, she saw the billboard.

The *Dead Man's Chest*
Davy Jones' Finest Saloon
Debauchery Guaranteed
You will not be disappointed

Debauchery guaranteed! She shook her head sadly. No wonder they had only one supporter on this forsaken planet. Clearly, the other females were so oppressed that they had become mere playthings. She walked further into town, ignoring the leering gazes of the males who sat idly along the sidewalk. Then, at a crossroads, her jaw dropped as she gazed upwards at a billboard.

The Courthouse
Her Honor Judge Malignia Maleficia
Libertania's Strictest Judge
Justice As You Need It – Hot and Strong and Severe
Hanging and Flaying a Speciality

She struggled to make sense of the picture of a female in leather jumpsuit and thigh-length boots, wielding a whip. Was it an icon of female strength and domination or an appalling depiction of the worst of male fantasies? There was only one way to find out. She walked up to the door under the billboard and knocked.

She found herself looking down at a hunched figure who regarded her suspiciously.

"Yeth?"

"I wish to talk to Judge Maleficia."

The figure became more suspicious.

"Why you want to talk to Her Honor?"

Junipa bristled.

"If you don't mind me saying so, it's none of your business. Is she here?"

Just then a voice boomed out.

"Who is it, Bruno?"

"Ith someone say they want to talk to you, Your Honor. Is female, I think. Shall I tell her to go away?"

"No, wait."

Junipa was taken aback as she saw something emerge from the gloom of the interior. It was at least a head taller than her, and clad all in leather. It had long, swept-back hair, dark gimlet-like eyes and a large, slightly aquiline nose. Not at all what she expected a judge to look like.

"Are you Judge Maleficia?"

"Yes. What is it you want?"

Junipa hesitated. She was used to dealing with females who were oppressed, downtrodden, in thrall to any number of male hegemonies, and who needed support and encouragement to oppose them. One look told Junipa that, whatever reason the Judge had for supporting the Feminarchs, being downtrodden was not one of them. She needed to tread carefully.

"Could we talk in private?"

The Judge waved a hand, in which Junipa noted she held a whip.

"Oh, don't mind Bruno. He never takes any notice of anything."

Juno looked again at Bruno and thought that was probably true. She decided to press on.

"My name is Junipa Penthiliopesdotter. I'm a representative of the Feminarchs."

There was a swift reaction. The Judge kicked Bruno and sent him sprawling.

"Bruno, go and clean the cage. It's filthy." Taking Junipa's arm, she led her inside. "Come in, my dear. I think we need to talk in private. I like to think that I'm one of your biggest supporters and, though I say so myself, I do my bit to keep these males from walking all over us."

As they entered Junipa, found herself staring at the array of whips, shackles and other implements lining the walls and at the chair with its straps.

"For my clients," said the Judge. "I pride myself on catering for every taste in self-humiliation."

"Are they all male?" asked Junipa, hardly able to believe her eyes.

"Of course, my dear," answered the Judge. "No female would put up with what I do to them. The more I lash them, the more they beg for it."

For few moments, Junipa felt an erotic charge, as she contemplated the idea of submissive males. The idea that at least some males had secret urges to abase themselves had never occurred to her. It needed further thought and maybe a whole new theoretical approach. However, that could wait. She had to attend to business.

"I am hoping that you may be able to help us in a matter that it is not an exaggeration to say is of Galactic importance. We are looking for a number of individuals who we believe have come to Libertania."

The Judge's eyebrows rose vertiginously.

"Most interesting. Do you think they may have come here?"

Junipa considered the idea of either de la Beche or Sloakum submitting to the Judge's attentions, and thought probably not.

"I doubt it, but I was hoping that with your, er, contacts, you might have picked up something."

The Judge gave a loud, braying laugh.

"My clients have very few secrets by the time I'm finished with them. I beat all their dirty little secrets out of them. They love to tell me everything. I couldn't stop them if I wanted to."

Junipa tried hard to suppress another erotic frisson.

"That could be very helpful. We are looking for three individuals by the names of Sloakum, Gulliver and de la Beche."

The Judge's eyes lit up.

"Do you mean Captain de la Beche? Why hadn't you mentioned him before? Such a refined and sensitive person. Quite unlike most of the riff-raff you get in this place. He has been here – not as a client of course," she said, as Junipa's face registered astonishment, "but as a guest, with his young assistant, Jim."

"Really? Do you know where he went after he left you?"

"I expect he went back to work on his opera."

Junipa looked at her, uncomprehending.

"His opera?"

The Judge tutted.

"Yes, his opera. Didn't you know about it? He is hoping to finish Handel's great unfinished work, *Oedipus Rex*. It's bound to take the Galaxy by storm. He and I are absolute devotees of Handel. I hope you are not going to interrupt him." she added. "He has promised to invite me to the premiere."

Junipa had only the faintest idea of what the Judge was talking about, but the de la Beche trail was now warm indeed. She needed to follow it.

"Where do you think he has gone to finish his opera?"

"He didn't say, but he is a captain, so he must have a ship. I expect he will be there."

Maybe the trail wasn't so warm. What about the others?

"Have you also heard of Captain Sloakum or Maggie Gulliver?"

The Judge shook her head.

"No. Are they friends of Captain de la Beche? Fellow Handel devotees, perhaps?"

Junipa could not hide a smile.

"Anything but," I'm afraid. "They are rather dangerous individuals. If you do hear anything of them, please contact me immediately. These are my communicator details. Now, if you'll excuse me, I have to go."

The Judge took her arm.

"Good luck with your mission, my dear. Give my regards to Captain de la Beche if you meet him." She picked up a whip and handed it to her. "Take this. You'll be surprised at the pleasure it gives."

28

Sloakum strode through the entrance to the *Dead Man's Chest* brandishing his cutlass at the doorman, who shrank back, unsure of what it was, but sure that he did not want to find out. Maggie swept in behind Sloakum. They found themselves in the long bar. A few of the customers showed a desultory interest in their appearance, but the rest carried on with what they were doing.

"Let's get ourselves a drink," said Sloakum. They sat at a table and he called over a potboy, who was wiping the tables. "Do ye have ale in this fleapit?"

The potboy trembled, unable to look them directly in the face. "Yes we do. Do you want our house ale or one of the specials?"

Sloakum snorted.

"None of yer fancy stuff. Just bring us ale."

The potboy nodded.

"Two glasses?"

Sloakum snorted again, more loudly.

"Two glasses! I want a drink, not something that wouldn't dampen me whiskers. Bring us six and have half a dozen more ready, 'cos they won't have long to wait."

The potboy scurried off and soon returned with a tray filled with large glasses. Sloakum picked up one and poured it straight down his throat. Maggie followed suit. Their seconds followed immediately. As he put down his second glass, Sloakum saw that the potboy was still standing there.

"What are ye waiting for, ye spavined midget? Bring us more, else we'll die of thirst."

The potboy hurried off. Maggie looked round the bar, unimpressed with what she saw.

"Look at 'em, Jonah Sloakum. Drunk, dead drunk or as good as dead. Ye'll learn nothing here."

Sloakum grunted, unable to disagree. The potboy returned, and as he was putting down the tray, one of the customers came over to their table.

"Pardon me for interrupting, but did I hear right? Are you the famous Captain Sloakum?"

Sloakum eyed him suspiciously.

"What's it to ye?"

"The name's Jake Kidney. I once sailed with Captain Lightfoot. We used to hear tales of you."

"Lightfoot? Never heard of him. What'd he do?" said Sloakum sniffily.

Jake Kidney seemed surprised.

"We took a good few prizes, mainly out Denebian way. Then we got caught. The Denebians didn't take too kindly to the ways of Captain Lightfoot. He was strung up for all to see and the same fate was in store for me too, only a couple of us managed to escape and get here. I've been here ever since and, truth to tell, I'm feeling bored. I could do with a little excitement, so I'm looking for a ship to join and thought maybe you could do with a hand."

Sloakum gave a derisive snort.

"I don't take the cast-offs of some labberneck of a captain bone-headed enough to get caught. We want hands that don't get caught on my ship."

Jake Kidney nodded.

"I know what you're thinking, but it wasn't like that with me. I told Captain Lightfoot not to try to take that last prize. I told him it was a trap, but he wouldn't have it and so we walked right into it. The Denebians were waiting for us. Besides, I have a little bit of information that I think you might be interested in. Take me on and I'll tell you more."

Sloakum was less than intrigued.

"Don't tell me. Ye know where Lightfoot stashed his loot. I've heard that story a million times."

Kidney shook his head.

"Not *his* loot, but maybe yours. I'll give you just two words – Dick McGoon."

The effect was instantaneous. Sloakum rose, incandescent with fury, spitting and waving his cutlass.

"Where'd ye hear that name? Spill yer guts now or I'll spill 'em for ye."

Kidney shrank back, alarmed.

"Easy now, Captain, easy. Let me put you in the picture. Me and Dick were drinking pals a long way back. He told me what he'd done when he sailed with you and I thought you might like a chance to get your own back."

Sloakum's fury subsided only a little.

"Where's that scurvy spawn of a twopenny whore now? Tell me now or ye'll be carrion for every fly on this godforsaken dunghill of a planet."

Kidney recovered some nerve.

"Let's not fall out, Captain. Dick don't come here no more. Take me on and I'll tell you where he is. I'll even take you there myself. You'll never find him otherwise."

29

Junipa was unsure of her next move. She was sitting on a bench looking at a patch of dusty ground which a nearby notice proclaimed was "Davy Jones Memorial Park". She was musing idly what exactly it was supposed to be memorialising when she heard a bleep from her communicator. She picked it up and was startled to see who was calling.

"Junipa," boomed a voice that set the instrument vibrating in her hand, "this is Judge Maleficia. I have news for you. Sloakum is here."

"What? With you?"

Try as she might, Junipa found it almost impossible to conjure up a vision of Sloakum submitting to the ministrations of the Judge.

"No, of course not," replied the Judge, evidently annoyed. "Do you imagine I would allow his sort here? No, I heard it from one of my clients, a very low, rascally fellow named Jake Kidney. He claims that he met Sloakum and he was about to join his crew."

"Are you sure?" asked Junipa sceptically. "And if you are, where is Sloakum now?"

"Oh, I am sure," replied the Judge. "I thrashed Kidney within an inch of his life and I know I got everything out of him. He was so pleased, he paid me double. He told me that he has promised to take Sloakum to the abode of another villainous creature, one Dick McGoon. Apparently, McGoon stole from Sloakum and now Sloakum wants retribution. I believe they are due to set off very soon."

Junipa was puzzled. If Sloakum was supposed to be hunting de la Beche, why was he going after this McGoon? Was it simply revenge, or was there something more to it? You could never tell with Sloakum. She needed to find out more.

"Do you know where McGoon's place is?"

"No, it seems he keeps it very well hidden, presumably to avoid the likes of Sloakum. All I know is that it is somewhere up in the mountains. I think Kidney must be one of the very few who knows where it is."

"How are they getting there?"

"The only way is on foot. The paths are so narrow and rutted that nothing on wheels could get there and you must have noticed that there are no flying vehicles to be seen. It's almost impossible to get spare parts here. I believe it would take several hours to get there."

Junipa considered her options.

"Do you think I could follow them without them seeing me?"

There was silence for a few seconds before the Judge answered.

"You could be taking your life in your hands. Once in the mountains, there is cover, but the bushes are very thorny and then there are the flies and the rats. It could be very uncomfortable."

"Rats?"

"Yes, vicious creatures, so I'm told."

Junipa did not like the sound of that at all. She had a phobia about rodents, particularly rats. Not exactly becoming for a Feminarch, but there it was. She decided to face her fear.

"Do you know when they plan to start?"

"Within the hour, I believe. They are going to meet at the *Dead Man's Chest*. It's a tavern; you have probably seen it."

***

Maggie Gulliver stood outside the *Dead Man's Chest*, shaking her fist at Sloakum while Jake Kidney looked on.

"Why do we have to go off traipsing in them there mountains? I thought we were supposed to be finding Fancypants? I hate walking and I hate the heat and I hate flies and I hate everything about this place and I always hated ye."

Being emollient did not come easy to Sloakum. In fact, it didn't come at all. Emollience was the last thing called for on any ship he captained. All he could do was bluster.

"He did the dirty on me, Maggie. He ran off with me treasure chest. No man does that and lives. Ye can stay here if ye likes, but I've sharpened the cutlass and, if ye come, I'll show ye the finest bit of gizzard-slittin ye'll ever see."

He knew Maggie could never resist a bit of bloodletting. Grumpily, she assented. From behind a wooden fence on the other side of the street, Junipa watched through a gap in the boards as the three began walking on the road out of town towards the far-off mountains. The country through which they were walking was only sparsely dotted with low thorn bushes, so she waited until they were almost out of sight before following. On the screen of her communicator, with the magnification set to maximum, she could see them trudging steadily along without looking back, swatting continuously at the flies. Often, Maggie appeared to be making gestures of annoyance at Sloakum.

After about an hour they started to ascend. The temperature began to drop, the bush became thicker and taller and the road petered out into a narrow, winding track. Junipa closed the distance between them. By now she was catching only glimpses of them through the scrub, but had no difficulty in following them, because of the noise they were making: a combination of Maggie's almost continual complaints and an occasional staccato grunt from Sloakum. Turning a sharp corner on the path she almost stumbled over the decapitated body of an animal. Its head lay just further up the path. She realized it must be one the rats that the Judge had mentioned. Just then, another rat appeared, sniffed at the body and then, as if alarmed, scurried squeaking back into the bush. She trudged on. A little later, she came across the body of another decapitated rat and, seeing how clean the cut had been, she knew it was the work of Sloakum's cutlass.

For hours they ascended, as the path became steeper and narrower. Every so often, Junipa would come across the body of a rat, almost as if they were signposts. Then the terrain levelled out a little, and she realized that the party had come to a halt a short way ahead. She stepped off the path and moved very slowly and carefully through the bushes towards them, in an effort to hear what they were saying. As she did so, there was a sudden loud squeak and a rustling noise and she heard Sloakum's voice.

"What was that? Maybe someone's following us?"

"It's probably one of them rats running away before ye chop its head off," said Maggie.

Heart pounding, Junipa retreated as carefully as she could further into the bushes and crouched down. Through gaps in the leaves, she could see Sloakum walking back along the path before turning and rejoining Maggie.

"Maybe ye're right, Maggie. Them rats don't like a taste of my cutlass."

Sloakum and Maggie had stopped just before a narrow opening in the bushes, through which Junipa could see a clearing.

"Dick's place is just through there," said Jake Kidney, "but you had best be careful. He can be a bit unfriendly, if you know what I mean."

"I'll give him unfriendly," said Sloakum. "I want ye to go in there and get him out, then I'll slit him from stern to bowsprit."

She could detect more than a hint of hesitation in Kidney's response.

"Ooh, I don't know about that. You see, me and Dick didn't exactly part on good terms. He said I was cheating at the card game I was running, because he was always losing. Not a bit of it. I didn't have to cheat, because he was useless at cards. That's why he always lost. But he wouldn't have it. So I barred him from the game and he vowed he would get his own back, one day."

Sloakum appeared to be unmoved.

"Whatever Dick McGoon will do to ye, it'll be nothing as to what I'll do, so get in there."

There was a pause. Then Junipa heard Maggie.

"Will ye two sort yerselves out, or I'll go in and do him meself!"

There came much angry muttering before Kidney finally spoke.

"I'll do it, I'll do it, but don't blame me if he cuts up rough."

She watched as Kidney went through to the clearing.

"Hello Dick, are you there? It's your old pal, Jake Kidney. I've brought someone with me that I think you know."

A few seconds later she heard angry shouting, followed by a loud bang as Kidney dived back through the opening and rolled over several times. He picked himself up and gingerly rubbed his leg.

"I told you he would cut up rough. He fired something at me. I could feel whatever it was go right past my ear."

She heard more snorting and muttering from Sloakum before she saw him march through the opening, waving his cutlass.

"Dick McGoon, ye know who I am and I'm here to get ye for what ye did. Come out and show yerself and fight proper or I'll come in and tickle yer cowardly, lyin' carcass with this."

She decided she needed a better view and wriggled her way through the bushes. In the clearing she could see a rundown wooden shack. A window in an upstairs room was flung open and a face appeared.

"I used to say, Sloakum, that if I ever saw ye again it would be too soon, but now I've changed my mind. One blast from this, and ye're good only for feeding to dogs, but dying quick is too good for ye. I want to enjoy meself and see ye go slow and painful."

There was another bang and a startled Sloakum grabbed the arm holding the cutlass. When he took his hand away, there was blood on it.

"It's me doing the tickling now, Sloakum. Plenty more to come before ye breathe yer last."

Just then, Junipa heard another voice.

"Enough, Dick McGoon! Enough. I want a word with ye."

Silence. Then the reply came, plaintive this time rather than angry.

"Is that really ye, Maggie? Have ye come back to me, after all this time?"

Junipa saw that Maggie was standing next to Sloakum and looking up at the window.

"I never was with ye in the first place, Dick McGoon, 'cept when I was too young to care and too drunk to think."

There was a muffled sob from the window.

"How can ye say that, Maggie? Ye were the only one I ever loved."

"I was never much of a one for love, Dick McGoon. I dallied with ye once; that I admit. But I was a young fool then and ye're an old fool now."

Another sob came from the window.

"And is Sloakum yer swain now, Maggie? Are ye sweet on him?"

Maggie gave a great belly-laugh.

"Ye're an even bigger fool than I took ye for, Dick McGoon. Do ye think I'd be sweet on this pustulous sack of slime?"

Sloakum grunted in annoyance as McGoon responded.

"I've thought of ye often, Maggie. There was never another for me after ye. My only pal is Maggie the cat, and I've named her after ye. I've been here on my own for a long time and that's the way I like it, except lately I've been pestered by Sloakum and his pox-ridden crew."

"Who are ye calling pox-ridden, Dick McGoon?"

"No, not ye, Maggie. I was talking about that bilge rat, Ben Bones. He was here. He used to sail with Sloakum. Ask him."

Maggie turned to Sloakum, who grunted in assent.

"What was he doing here?" asked Maggie.

"He was with a few others. The one in charge called himself Captain and had a funny name – and he dressed funny too."

Junipa could see both Maggie and Sloakum react in surprise.

"Was he called de la Beche?" asked Maggie.

"Yes. That's the one. I told ye he had a funny name."

"Where did he go from here?"

"He didn't say, but I guess he went back to town."

"What did he want?"

"Ye won't believe this, but he wanted to know how to get to Utrophia."

Maggie gasped in surprise, while Sloakum spat twice on the ground saying, "Ye don't say that word lest ye want to cross Lady Luck, McGoon."

"Why would he ask ye?" said Maggie.

"Because I went there once."

Sloakum spat on the ground again. Maggie shook her head in astonishment.

"Nobody's supposed to know how to get there. How come ye did?"

"It's a long story Maggie. We had this ball."

"A ball?"

"Yes. It had funny writing on it and my first mate, Jason, reckoned it might mean something, so he took it to the Coders, pointy heads that live in the town, and they deciphered it for him. Turns out that it was directions to get to Utrophia. So we decided to go. We thought they would just be a load of god-botherers and there would be easy pickings. It was anything but. We were set upon by a load of mad monks and only just saved our skins."

"So where is this ball now?"

"De la Beche has it."

"Ye gave it to him?"

"I didn't want to, but he got me all befuddled. It won't do him any good though. It was dead."

Maggie pondered this news.

"He's a crafty one, from what I hear. I wouldn't put it past him to bring it back from the dead. Did ye tell him about these Coders?"

"I dunno, Maggie. My mind was so befuddled I might have."

"If ye did, he would take it to them. Then he'd be off to Utrophia, though why he would want to go, beats me. If we don't get him here, maybe we could catch him there. Is that ball the only way to get there?"

There was a long pause before McGoon answered.

"Since ye ask, Maggie, there is another way. We went in my last ship, the *Molly Malone*, best ship I ever had. More fool me, I lost her at a game of cards, but before I let her go, Jason copied all her systems for me. There were a lot of things I wanted to see and do if I ever got another ship."

"Ye'll let me have it Dick, won't ye?" said Maggie in an appealing tone.

"I can't, Maggie. Ye know I'd give ye anything, but it won't work without me. That's the way Jason and me set it up. We didn't want anyone to get their thieving paws on it."

Maggie turned to Sloakum and muttered something that Junipa could not catch. She looked back up at McGoon.

"Ye'll have to come with us then, Dick."

McGoon's reaction was half laugh, half snort.

"I ain't going nowhere with Sloakum, Maggie. Ye must know that."

Maggie was undaunted.

"There's gold in it for ye, Dick McGoon. Ye were always partial to gold."

There was a long wait before McGoon replied.

"What sort of gold, Maggie?"

"Proper gold, Dick, doubloons. There's five hundred for ye if ye come with us and we catch Fancypants de la Beche."

Another long pause followed.

"How can I trust ye, Maggie?"

"I'll make ye the Pirate Promise, Dick."

"What about Sloakum?"

"He's made it with me, Dick. Ye make it with me and it's good for all three of us."

Junipa watched as McGoon's face disappeared from the window. A few moments later, he came out of the door. They each spat in their hands and then McGoon walked towards Maggie and they held their palms together. From somewhere, there came into her mind a half-remembered piece of pirate lore: no one ever breaks the Pirate Promise.

30

Jim watched from the rear of the *Bountiful*'s Bridge as de la Beche and Mr Betelgeuse examined the ball, which still appeared lifeless. Around them, other members of the crew looked on. De la Beche put the ball down on the table and shook his head.

"We haven't managed to get so much as a peep out of it, I'm afraid."

"That's Dick McGoon for yer, Cap'n," said Bosun Bones, "He never was one for giving anything away. Always a tightwad he was. I've got an idea. Why don't we give Doris a try? She can get anything to talk."

De la Beche nodded.

"Go ahead. Nothing ventured."

Bosun Bones tapped Doris, who uttered a series of squeaks and whistles. Jim said he thought that he saw a flicker of light on the surface of the ball, but the others said they saw nothing. Doris tried again. This time, Jim was convinced that he saw something, but again the others did not.

"Maybe your young eyes are better than ours, Jim, but I think there is only one thing for it. We will have to go back to the Coders. Perhaps they can do something."

***

Wearied from the heat and the flies, the trio trudged back to Davey Jones. Sloakum mopped his brow with a large red and white spotted kerchief. "I need a drink, Maggie, else I'll die of thirst." He marched into the *Dead Man's Chest*, brandishing his cutlass at the cowering doorman. Maggie and McGoon followed close behind. They sat at a table as the potboy came over."Ales all round," said Sloakum, "and keep 'em coming till I say stop – and I ain't goin' to say stop anytime soon."

For several rounds, silence reigned. Talking, in Sloakum's opinion, interfered with the serious business of drinking. After several rounds, Maggie finally decided to speak.

"I do like a drop, Jonah Sloakum, but we ain't goin' to find Fancypants de la Beche just sittin' here quaffin' ale."

Sloakum snorted and picked up a glass that the potboy had just delivered. The potboy looked at Sloakum and Maggie, as if wanting to say something.

"Lookin for a tip, are ye?" said Maggie. "Ye'll get nothing from him."

"No," replied the potboy. "I heard you talking about Captain de la Beche. Are you a friend of his?"

Sloakum grunted.

"I ain't got no friends round here."

"Nor nowhere else," said Maggie with a guffaw.

The potboy seemed surprised.

"Well, he's here. I saw him a little while ago on my way in."

Sloakum sat up with a start, slamming his glass down and spraying some of its contents over the table.

"D'ye know where he was going?"

The potboy said he had no idea.

"He can't have gone far," said Maggie. "Now's our chance to nab him."

Sloakum shook his head.

"Nah, he might have some of his crew with him. We don't know what they're like. I told ye we'll need more of us. I'll get 'em down here from the ship."

Maggie seemed doubtful.

"Are ye sure that scurvy bunch are up for it?"

"If it's for fightin', there's nothin' they like better. Besides, I'll have any shirker strung up." He put his hand in his pocket, pulled out a battered communicator and barked an order. "Get Poison Pete. Tell him to get a posse together and get down here. Only bring clubs and knives. We don't want hotheads firing off blasters and shooting our golden goose."

***

Jim was utterly bemused by his change of surroundings. One moment he was in bright sunlight, outside the Tesseract with the others. The next he was in deep gloom. In his hand was the ball that de la Beche had asked him to hold while he was searching for any sign of an entrance. Gradually, the gloom began to lift a little and he could see he was in a large windowless room. On the far wall he could just make out some lettering.

There is an infinity of dimensions; not all are real

There is an infinity of realities; not all have dimensions

He realized he was back in the Tesseract. Then he saw the figure of Grosse Calabi-Yau becoming slowly visible.

"You again?" said Grosse languidly. "I thought you had had enough."

"I have had more than enough," said Jim, "infinitely more, after the last time. I have no idea how I came to be here but, since I am, I wish to see the Coders."

"Do you indeed?" said Grosse. "You make very bold for one so small and lacking in dimensions."

"At least all my dimensions are visible," retorted Jim, his resentment at Grosse's attitude rapidly rising. "I can only see two of yours. You say the rest are curled up, but how do I know they even exist? I think you're just a flattie."

"A what?" said Grosse, in a surprised tone of voice.

"A flattie. A two-dimensional wisp, all surface, no substance."

"Two are quite enough to treat with the likes of you," said Grosse. "I reserve my other dimensions for my dealings with more important personages."

"Really?" said Jim, scornfully. "And who might these more important personages be?"

"Personages far too important for me to name," said Grosse. "Practically all the important personages there are or could be. They would be appalled at the thought of my discussing them with your sort."

"Is that so?" said Jim. "Perhaps I could suggest a few names of importance for you. How about the Drogon of Arithmethetea?"

"I have the honour of Her Magnficence's acquaintance," replied Grosse, in what Jim thought was a distinctly pompous tone.

"And the Grand Vizier of Despotica?"

"His Grandiloquence has bestowed on me the signal honour of Knight Commander of the Order of the Sunbeam Talbot."

"My congratulations," said Jim, "and I suppose you know the Hundred Snellnooks of the Halls of Croesovia?"

Grosse's eyes narrowed.

"I have of course met many of their Excellencies. I hope to have the pleasure of meeting others very soon."

"Hah!" said Jim, a note of triumph creeping into his voice. "Now I know you are a fraud. They don't exist, and even if they did, they would all have been slain by my friend, the Bold Deceiver."

Grosse did not seem the least put out.

"They may not exist in your dimensionally impoverished universe," he said dismissively, "but I can assure you that they can all be found in the many more dimensions that I have at my disposal. I can quite understand why they wouldn't bother coming down to your level."

Jim decided he had had enough. He stamped his foot.

"I've had enough of this nonsense. I wish to see the Coders. Please take me to them."

"Temper, temper," said Grosse. "Behaving like that will get you nowhere. Why do you wish to see them?"

"I have this ball. I believe it's full of secrets that only they can interpret."

"They wouldn't be in the least interested in a silly ball. They don't play games, you know." He made a snuffling sound that Jim thought might be a laugh. "What do you want to talk to them about?"

"Utrophia."

Grosse looked at him very suspiciously.

"Why do you want to ask about that?"

Jim held up the ball.

"Look, there's nothing on it now, but I am told that the last message on it was 'Seek ye Roy Pesshe'. You told me last time that 'Roy Pesshe' was a clue to finding Utrophia."

Grosse said nothing and then slowly began to fade away.

Jim looked around. The room was now bare and empty and even gloomier. Even the slogan had disappeared from the wall. Then the light became brighter and the walls a rather pleasant pastel shade of cream.

"What can I do for you?"

The voice came from behind. He turned round and saw a figure sitting in an elaborately-carved high-backed chair. He appeared to be quite old, with a bald head and a long, luxuriant grey beard.

At first, Jim was so startled he could not speak, but eventually he managed to regain his composure.

"What happened to Grosse?"

The figure smiled benignly.

"Gone for the moment. I'm afraid Grosse sometimes gets wrapped up in himself."

"Something to do with all his dimensions?" asked Jim.

"Indeed. I've spoken to him about that before. He needs to come out of himself a bit more. Unwrap a few of those dimensions and discard the others. He'll enjoy things so much more. It's a much more common problem than you might think," he added. "That's what happened to Gravity."

"Gravity?" said Jim, completely bemused.

"Yes, Gravity," came the reply. "It insists on spreading itself across extra dimensions. Quite unnecessary, and as a result, it is very weak. It happens to a lot of things. You would be surprised."

Jim had to admit to himself that he was surprised and not a little puzzled.

"What do you mean, weak?"

Now it was the man's turn to look surprised.

"You must know Gravity is very weak compared to other forces like Electromagnetism and Nuclear. Mighty fellows, those. Gravity you hardly notice. It's all to do with octonions, you see."

Jim didn't see.

"What are octonions?"

The old man sighed.

"I thought you would ask me that. They're a bit like numbers, only they're very complex. You have to multiply them in the right way, otherwise you get things wrong. You can get a lot wrong with gravity."

Jim could remember that he had fallen foul of the laws of gravity on more than one occasion, and had felt that he, rather than gravity, was the weaker of the two, but felt that it was not the time to pursue that line of thought. He decided to return to the task in hand.

"I was looking for the Coders. Can you take me to them?"

The man gave another benign smile.

"I am the Coders."

Jim was puzzled. He had assumed Coders was plural.

"Is there just one of you?"

"That depends. How many did you want?"
"It's not a question of what I want. I thought there must be more

of you because ..." he had to think some more, "because, for a start, you order lots of pizzas."

The figure nodded.

"Ah yes, pizzas. Such serviceable meals. They are thin, so they slide easily between dimensions, you see. The same, alas, can't be said for some other dishes. Victoria sponge, for example, never has quite the same texture in other dimensions. Such a pity. I'm very fond of a Victoria sponge."

For a moment, Jim tried to imagine a multi-dimensional Victoria sponge, but then gave up. He thought, too, about asking him how he could be more than one Coder, but decided that would be wasting time. Best to get straight to the point.

"'Seek ye Roy Pesshe'. What does that mean?"

No response came. Jim realized that the room was becoming darker again and the old man was disappearing from view. Just as it became so dark that he could see nothing, there was an almost blinding flash of light and he found himself looking at a kaleidoscope of images on a screen that surrounded him on all sides. He saw massed ranks of soldiers marching in perfect unison; orators declaiming to huge crowds; massive explosions sending clouds of debris like mushrooms high into the air; a vast, muddied plain on which were strewn what appeared to be innumerable bodies; the faces of males, females and children beside destroyed buildings, all accompanied by the sounds of deafening explosions, wailing sirens and shouts and screams in languages he did not understand. Suddenly the entire screen froze and on it appeared:

Who will lead you into the bliss of ignorance?

The soundtrack became a low, rhythmic chant. On the screen, a figure appeared, dressed in a white smock that extended down to his feet. He began to speak.

> The spirit of curiosity is not a good spirit. It is the spirit of dispersion, of distancing oneself from God, the spirit of talking too much. This spirit of curiosity, which is worldly, leads us to confusion.

The screen divided and a plump figure dressed all in black, with a floppy cap, banged a fist angrily on a table.

> Reason is the Devil's greatest whore; by nature and manner of being, she is a noxious whore; she is a prostitute, the Devil's appointed whore; a whore eaten by scab and leprosy, who ought to be trodden under foot and destroyed, she and her wisdom.

The screen divided again, showing an ascetic-looking male in a high-winged collar and tight-fitting jacket looking sternly ahead.

> The land that we dreamed of would be the home of a people who valued knowledge only as a basis for right living, of a people who devoted their leisure to the things of the spirit – a land whose countryside would be bright with cosy homesteads, whose fields and villages would be joyous with the romping of sturdy children, the contest of athletic youths and the laughter of happy maidens, whose firesides would be forums for the wisdom of serene old age. The home, in short, of a people living the life that God desires that they should live.

Then all three disappeared and a single image remained of a white-haired male with a goatee beard, wearing wire-rimmed spectacles and a wide-brimmed hat.

> Sometimes it happens that a man's circle of horizon becomes smaller and smaller, and as the radius approaches

zero, it concentrates on one point. And then that becomes his point of view.

The screen went black and the room was dark once more. Then the lights slowly raised, and Jim could see that the old man was still sitting in his chair.

"What was that all about?" asked Jim, completely bemused by what he had seen.

"It's the Panalecton. What would you like it to be about about?" replied the old man.

"That's not the point," replied Jim. "Do you always answer a question with another question?"

The old man smiled.

"Surely you agree that questions are much more certain than answers?"

"I'm not sure I do," said Jim. "In fact, I don't think I understand what you mean."

"Well, answers are always questionable, but if you say a question is answerable, then it's not really a question at all, because the answer is already known."

Jim thought he saw a flaw in the logic.

"What if I ask a question to which there is no answer?"

"Well, then it's a riddle. I must say I prefer riddles, don't you?"

Jim shook his head in exasperation.

"No, I don't. Do you always talk in riddles?"

"What else is there?"

Jim's exasperation increased.

"Lots of things. For one, do you know about the Panalecton?"

The old man hesitated a little before he answered.

"What do you want to know?"

"Is it true that it contains all knowledge?"

"Yes and no."

Jim threw up his hands.

"Why can you never give a straight answer? Either it does or it doesn't."

"Not at all," said the old man. "If the Panalecton contains all knowledge, then it must itself be knowledge. So does it contain itself? If it does not, then it does not contain all knowledge, and if it does, then what contains it must also be knowledge and therefore it does not contain all knowledge. You do see my point?"

Jim didn't think he did. Instead he felt a curious sensation, as if he was going down a rabbit hole in his mind. He decided to change the subject.

"What about Roy Pesshe? I mention those words and suddenly all that stuff appears on the screen."

The old man nodded sympathetically.

"Yes, I agree it must have been rather puzzling. You saw it in only two dimensions. It is clearer in five, especially with octonion dimensions."

"Then can I see it in five?"

"No."

"Why not?"

"Because you barely have three, none with octonions."

Jim thought he would try one last avenue.

"Is Roy Pesshe part of the Panalecton?"

"Yes and no."

Jim was running out of patience. "What excuse are you going to give me this time?"

"'Seek ye Roy Pesshe.' Seek and you may find the answer."

"And what about you? Are you part of the Panalecton? Don't tell me," he added. "Yes and no."

The old man smiled.

"I believe you have something for me."

Jim blinked and then remembered the original reason that they had come to the Tesseract. He handed him the ball.

The old man examined it carefully.

"I have seen one of these before. How did you find it?"

Jim told him of the events with Dick McGoon.

"Ah yes. We had to extract some information from it. It was mostly directions to a certain place, from what I remember."

"To Utrophia?" asked Jim.

"Yes, to Utrophia. Not a place everyone would care to visit."

Jim stared at the ball.

"It doesn't seem to be working now."

The old man put it on a pad on a table next to his chair.

"It just needs refreshing. It shouldn't take very long. What do you want to do with it?"

"Well, we were also hoping to go to Utrophia."

"We?"

"Yes. I'm with Captain de la Beche and his crew." He looked around but saw no one else. "They came with me but they don't seem to be here now."

The old man nodded.

"Yes, I believe they are being entertained elsewhere." He handed Jim the ball. "I think this is working now. If you go through there you will find them."

Jim turned to see a door in the opposite wall. He turned back to thank the old man, but he had disappeared. He walked through the door to find himself in a theatre. At one end was a stage on which he could see a number of music stands and de la Beche waving a baton.

"Ah, Jim. Where have you been? You've missed a treat. I have been working with a simply marvellous little chamber orchestra on the first act of my *Oedipus Rex*. We have come up with a beautifully grisly overture depicting the plague of Thebes and a nicely sinister theme for the seer Teiresias. I am sure George Frideric would approve. Don't you agree, Mr Betelgeuse?"

"I'm sure he would," said Mr Betelgeuse gravely.

"What about you, Sawbones? Have you enjoyed things?"

Jim saw that Doctor Culpepper was sitting beside a cabinet in which there was a row of bottles and several glasses.

"Top class, Sechy. Some of the finest whiskies here that I've tasted in a long time."

De la Beche smiled graciously. "The orchestra should be back soon. I can't wait to do some more."

Then, in an instant, the scene changed. They found themselves on the street looking up at the Tesseract. De la Beche shrugged.

"Oh well. I did wonder whether it was too good to last."

31

Her communicator beeped and Junipa saw that it was Judge Maleficia. She sounded agitated.

"Junipa, that ruffian Kidney has been back again, wanting to be thrashed out of his misery. You will remember that he told me that Sloakum had promised to take him on as crew after he had shown him where that other villain, McGoon, lived? Well, now he tells me that Sloakum has gone back on his word after they found McGoon, and he is very angry about it. Frankly, I care nothing for his feelings, but something else he told me did disturb me greatly. Apparently, Sloakum is here to try to capture Captain de la Beche. What do you make of that?"

Junipa hesitated, trying to think of the best way to put things.

"Yes, we did hear that he was up to something of the sort. He is also in cahoots with another notorious pirate, Maggie Gulliver."

"Why would they want the Captain? He is such a cultured person, quite unlike Sloakum or any of his cronies."

Junipa thought it best not to go into details.

"It's a bit complicated. Sloakum has been hired by another organization. I can't say too much at the moment."

There was a pause before the Judge replied.

"So you knew about it. Why didn't you say so?"

"Well, I didn't want to trouble you. As I said, this matter is very complicated and you had met de la Beche only once and quite by chance."

The communicator fairly rattled with the force of the Judge's response.

"Well now I *am* troubled. We must not allow Captain de la Beche to fall into the hands of those cutthroats. I shall make sure it does not happen."

"Pardon?"

"I shall take steps to rescue him."

Junipa could not quite believe what she had heard.

"How exactly could you do that, Your Honor?"

"I shall assemble a bodyguard of my clients."

Junipa just managed to stop herself from laughing out loud.

"I am sure you mean well, Your Honor, but – how can I put it – your clients are more used to obeying than resisting."

Again, Junipa felt the communicator rattle.

"*Exactly*. They will obey me when I tell them what they must do. Also, I have an inducement. My premium service is an exquisitely refined combination of torture and culture, administered with all my instruments, to the accompaniment of *Il Tricerbero Umiliato* from Handel's *Rinaldo*. It is normally reserved for very special clients on very special occasions and, as you might well imagine, there is a long waiting list. I shall offer one free session to all those who answer my call. I can assure you that there will be no shortage of takers."

Junipa was at a loss for words. The male psyche was even more bizarre than she had imagined, but the Judge clearly knew more about it than she ever would. Maybe it would work.

"Thank you, Your Honor. A most useful suggestion – but you would need to be quick."

"Of course. I shall instruct that rascal Kidney to round them up immediately. He might as well do something useful for once. We shall find Captain de la Beche and inform him that we Feminarchs are making ourselves responsible for his safety."

Junipa felt a sudden pang of alarm.

"No, no, you mustn't mention that we are involved. This is a most secret operation. The very survival of the Feminarchs depends on it. Just tell him you are doing it because you are fellow Handel-lovers."

***

As they stood outside the Tesseract, Jim watched as de la Beche examined the ball he held in his palm. Various symbols flashed over its surface, but nothing resembling "Seek ye Roy Pesshe". He handed it to Mr Betelgeuse, who held it close to a pen-like instrument.

"It does seem to be communicating some instructions, Captain, but it is difficult to tell with this. We would need to get it back to the ship to be sure."

"Let's do that. No point in wasting time here." De la Beche opened his communicator. "Gobby, darling, send the cutter down to pick us up."

Jim heard Gobby's voice crackle. "Bit of a problem with the cutter, Captain. We're fixing it now, but it might take a little while."

"How long is 'a little while'?"

"We'll know more in about an hour, Captain."

De la Beche sighed, then turned to the others. "While we're waiting we might as well return to the tavern for some refreshments."

As they entered the bar, Bosun Bones gave a sudden start. "Cap'n," whispered Bones, "ye won't believe this, but I've just seen Sloakum."

De la Beche looked at him sceptically.

"Are you sure?"

He nodded towards three figures hunched over their drinks in a dark corner of the bar.

"Look over there. No one don't never forget Sloakum, Cap'n – it's him alright, large as life and ten times as ugly. And look who he's with – Dick McGoon. I'd have thought Sloakum would have slit his gizzard after what he done – and the other is the spittin' image of Maggie Gulliver."

"The female pirate?" said de la Beche. "You know her?"

"Oh I know her alright," said Bones. "She and Sloakum go back a long way. Only it couldn't be her. She hates Sloakum because he did the dirty on her, and besides, she's been locked up for years by those Femmies."

De la Beche digested the news.

"I was told by Splenditheran that he had been sent to get me. I wonder how he knew we were here."

De la Beche turned to rest of the company.

"Well, darlings, there are five of us – six, if we include Jim. That should be more than enough to confront a trio of raddled has-beens. The Bold Deceiver alone has despatched a hundred times more in an afternoon. If Sloakum tries anything, we should be more than enough for him."

Jim looked at the faces of the company. Mr Betelgeuse was as inscrutable as ever; Doctor Culpepper looked apprehensive, while Bosun Bones had a rather sickly grin. Only the Bold Deceiver seemed enthusiastic. Just then, Sloakum looked up and, seeing them, leapt to his feet with a yell, brandishing his cutlass. Before any of them could move, Jim heard a loud noise from the entrance and the door swung open. Through it surged a dozen or more males, yelling and brandishing staves, knives and what looked like swords, scattering startled drinkers. Above the din, he could hear Sloakum yelling.

"Over here, ye scurvy sons of whores. What kept ye? Now do as I tell ye or I'll have ye skinned and fed to rats."

"We may be in a spot of bother. It looks like the odds have turned," said de la Beche, as he saw Sloakum's crew.

"Let's run for it," said Doctor Culpepper.

"Where to, Sawbones?" said de la Beche. "Until the cutter gets here, we haven't much hope of rescue. We will have to resist." He looked up at the bar wall. "Jim, grab those swords. They look as if they're sharp enough to do some damage."

Jim leapt up onto a table and tugged hard at a sword, which didn't move. Then he noticed a small catch at one end. He flipped it and the sword slid out. He released two more and tossed them down to de la Beche, the Doctor and Bosun Bones. As he did so, he could hear Sloakum shouting instructions.

"It's only Fancypants there I want and I want him alive and without a scratch. For the rest, slit every one of their pox-ridden gizzards."

The drinkers had retreated to the other end of the bar and, having recovered from their initial surprise, seemed to be watching what was happening as if it was something put on for their amusement. As they heard Sloakum speak, a cheer went up. It looked like the fun was going to begin.

As Sloakum's crew began to advance, de la Beche barked instructions.

"The Bold Deceiver, you and I will take the front. Sawbones, you and Bosun Bones guard our flanks. Mr Betelgeuse and Jim, hold our rear."

Jim, holding a large, heavy sword with both hands, stood trembling as Sloakum's crew advanced, led by a tall, scrawny figure waving a long-handled axe; he wore a red polka-dot bandanna and sported large scars on either cheek. As they came near, the Bold Deceiver leapt forward, rapier at the ready.

"Who dares challenge the Bold Deceiver? Step back, Sirrah, or prepare to meet your doom."

For a moment the figure stopped, then let out a guffaw.

"Poison Pete steps back for none. I'll give ye doom, ye spavined pipsqueak."

He raised his axe and Jim saw the Bold Deceiver dart forward with a flourish of his rapier in a blur of motion. Poison Pete swung his axe, but the Bold Deceiver stepped nimbly aside and flicked his rapier across the pirate's arm, drawing blood. Enraged, Poison Pete swung the axe wildly to and fro, as the Bold Deceiver skipped around him, taunting him with his rapier. Poison Pete let out a cry, dropped the axe and clutched his face. Jim could see blood trickling from his one eye. Then came another rapier thrust, this time deep into the crotch. Poison Pete fell to the floor writhing and screaming in agony. The rest of the crew hesitated. Then they heard Sloakum.

"What are ye waiting for, ye bilge-sucking, chicken-hearted scum?"

They started to advance again. Just then, Jim heard another commotion at the back of the bar. He turned to see drinkers being scattered by a figure clad in black leather wielding a whip. It was Her Honor, Judge Maleficia, followed by a score of others. Kicking more drinkers aside, she strode forward, as Sloakum's crew hesitated again.

"Captain de la Beche, are you being troubled by this disgraceful rabble?"

De la Beche gave an appreciative nod.

"They do seem to have taken against us, Your Honor. I can't imagine why."

The Judge glared at Sloakum's crew.

"I shall have to teach them that the Law is not to be taken lightly here."

She raised her whip and, with a flick of her wrist, it snaked out and wrapped itself around the neck of one of the crew. Another flick of the wrist sent his head back with a jerk and he fell to the ground, motionless. A low moan, that Jim thought was fear, went up from the rest of the crew.

"Now, you have a choice," said the Judge. "Be gone from here immediately and never return, or else face the most severe consequences. Believe me, I shall show no leniency when I sentence you."

The crew began to murmur among themselves. Then Jim heard Sloakum shout.

"Take no notice of that hoorie. Any that leaves without me saying so will leave without his skull."

The Judge wielded her whip again and another of Sloakum's crew fell, screaming and clutching his neck.

The murmurs grew louder and, above them, Jim heard a female voice.

"There's too many of 'em, Jonah Sloakum. We'll all leave here without our skulls if ye have yer way. Let's get out now, while we can. We'll have another day."

A stream of oaths erupted from Sloakum's mouth. His crew began to retreat towards the door, dragging Poison Pete and the whip victims with them. Jim watched as Maggie dragged Sloakum out by one arm, while the other brandished his cutlass. As the door closed behind them, Jim looked out of the bar window. He saw them clamber onto the back of a flatbed truck that had been standing outside. It sped off and, as it disappeared, he could see the figure of Sloakum, still waving his cutlass, doubtless still swearing retribution.

"I cannot thank you enough, Your Honor," said de la Beche. "You arrived in the nick of time. Things were beginning to look a bit tricky. How did you know?"

"I have my sources, Captain. People tell me things. I heard that Sloakum was up to no good here and I could not allow someone as cultured as yourself to fall into that oaf's hands. If I had, *Oedipus Rex* would never be finished. I simply could not allow that."

De la Beche gave a slight bow.

"Your Honor is more than kind. When *Oedipus Rex* is finished, as a small token of my gratitude, allow me to include a dedication to you in the first edition of the score."

The Judge clapped her hands and, as Jim thought, so far as she was capable of simpering, simpered.

"Oh, Captain de la Beche, I am quite overcome."

De la Beche smiled graciously. He was about to respond when one of the Judge's followers came up. The Judge beckoned him forward.

"Captain de la Beche, can I introduce Jake Kidney. He was the one who informed me of Sloakum's intentions."

De la Beche extended his hand.

"Very pleased to meet you, Mister Kidney, and many thanks, too."

"You're welcome, Captain. Anything to foil that lying blaggard Sloakum."

Turning to the Judge, he said, "I do hope our next session will be soon, Your Honor."

The Judge nodded assent.

"Of course, Jake Kidney, you are first on the list. Would you like to know what you will be getting?"

"Yes please, Your Honor."

The Judge addressed him sternly.

"First, to set the scene, you will receive a severe whipping. Then you will be offered a choice of chains, manacles or the electric chair. After that, comes the Rack and then, finally, the climax – the Iron Maiden. This will all be accompanied by music from George Frideric Handel's finest operas, including *Il Tricerbero Umiliato* from *Rinaldo."* Turning to de la Beche she said, "An idea has just occurred to me, Captain de la Beche. Perhaps, when you have finished *Oedipus Rex,* we could also include something from it?"

"Of course, Your Honor. I think an aria from the scene where Oedipus has his eyes gouged out would be suitable."

"Most appropriate, Captain. Now, Jake Kidney, that is what I have in store for you.

Jim saw Jake Kidney shiver a little with excitement.

"I can't tell you, Your Honor, how much I'm looking forward to it."

32

Jim had assumed his usual perch at the rear of the *Bountiful*'s Bridge and gazed at a large screen as data was being transferred from the ball to the ship's systems. Progress reports and images flitted intermittently-- across the screen until finally the process seemed to terminate.

"Well, Mr Betelgeuse," said de la Beche, "what have we got?"

Mr Betelgeuse started intently at the final screen.

"It does seem to have transferred navigational instructions, Captain."

"For Utrophia?"

"I do believe so, Captain."

"So now we know where we are going?"

Mr Betelgeuse continued to stare at the screen.

"This is a most interesting situation, Captain. Utrophia and its star are situated almost equidistantly between three stellar black holes. The resultant curvature of space means that electromagnetic radiation is deflected round them and Utrophia is effectively invisible to the rest of the Galaxy."

"So the rest of us don't know what they get up to?" said de la Beche.

"That may well be so, Captain. However, I would like to point out a problem. The disposition of the black holes makes selecting the correct hyperspace trajectory very problematic. Any slight error in the calculation might mean we have crossed an event horizon when we emerge and so disappear forever."

At that moment, McTavish chose to make an appearance.

"If ye think ah'm takin' ye there ye can boil yer hied."

"Oh come now, McTavish," said de la Beche. "It can't be that difficult. McGoon and his crew managed to get there and all those paragons of religion must have found a way, too."

"Aye. Mebbe they just put their hands together and prayed, but ah dinnae do that stuff."

De la Beche gave a dismissive wave.

"We know you have never met an expectation that you couldn't dash, McTavish, but on this occasion there is no choice. Prepare to take us to Utrophia – and beware of those black holes."

***

"Fancypants'll be half way there by now. We've got to follow him if we're ever going to get our hands on that gold ye keep promising me. What's the matter with ye, Jonah Sloakum? Frit are ye?"

Maggie Gulliver berated Sloakum as he sat slumped in his chair on the bridge of the *Rum, Sodomy and the Lash*.

"I ain't frit of no one, Maggie, but I don't hold with the sort found there, all dressed up in their fancy garbs. They ain't no friends of Lady Luck, that's for sure. The stories I've heard. Any dealings with them and before ye know it, ye're saying hello to Davy Jones."

"Ye are frit, Jonah Sloakum, and no mistake. Well I ain't – and we're going there, if I have to drive this ship meself. Who's the comms here?" She saw one of the crew shoot a glance at Sloakum, before pretending to study the screen in front of him. "Is that ye? What's yer name?"

More glances at Sloakum before the answer came.

"Sparky."

Maggie gave a snort.

"Well, Sparky, ye had better live up to yer name. Ye've a job to do. Dick McGoon, get yer lazy carcass over here."

McGoon, who had been lurking at the rear of the bridge, shuffled over.

"Show him yer stick."

McGoon handed Sparky a small cylindrical object. Sparky examined it.

"What am I supposed to do with this?"

"If ye get off yer pox-ridden rump, it'll tell ye how to get to Utrophia," said Maggie, "so get going."

Sparky looked disbelieving but set the cylinder down next to his screen. Immediately the screen began to flicker. He studied it for several seconds.

"Won't work. It's incompatible."

"What do yer mean?"

"It's incompatible. It talks a different language to our systems."

Maggie gave him her most intimidating glare.

"Yer head'll be incompatible with yer neck if ye don't get the two of them talking like lovebirds right now. Get to it."

A mixture of surprise and fear flickered over Sparky's face before he slumped down and, as Maggie stood looming over him, began issuing instructions. After several minutes, he looked up.

"Well?" said Maggie.

"I think it's working. We're getting something now."

Maggie's look was still intimidating.

"But are ye getting the way to Utrophia?"

Sparky shrugged.

"It looks like there's a lot of data there. It will take us a while to sort it out."

Maggie was not impressed.

"Ye don't have 'a while'. Me and the Captain are going to get us a drink. Ye'd better have it when we come back. Come on, Jonah Sloakum," she said, grabbing his arm. "Let's put some backbone in ye."

***

"We believe that de la Beche and Sloakum have both gone to Utrophia. What do you think we should do now?"

Junipa looked anxiously at Orestia, who appeared relaxed.

"I think you should go, too. You can keep an eye on them."

Junipa shook her head, nonplussed.

"I thought its location is a secret."

Junipa nodded.

"True, but one of our members, who has asked me that her name be kept secret, has so bewitched a particularly reactionary cleric of an appallingly unenlightened superstition that she has managed to get her hands on this." She handed a small, glassy ball to Junipa. "Our systems people have told me that it contained the instructions for navigation to Utrophia. They have transferred the information to the ship that will transport you."

Junipa's anxiety was beginning to edge into panic.

"I really don't think that's a good idea. For a start, they don't allow females there."

Something close to a smile played across Orestia's features.

"Well, you will have to disguise yourself as a male."

***

"Mister Betelgeuse. Have we obtained the coordinates for Utrophia?"

"Yes, Captain."

"Helmsman, prepare to set the course. I will give the customary orders. What wind do we have, Helmsman?"

"Freshening from east nor' east, Captain."

"And what sail?"

"Mainsail, foresail, main topsail and mizzen staysail, Captain."

"Hoist jib and moonraker."

"Do you think she can take it in this wind, Captain?"

"She can take it, Helmsman. Utrophia, here we come."

www.ingramcontent.com/pod-product-compliance
Lightning Source LLC
La Vergne TN
LVHW050629100826
845148LV00011B/1804